Wrapped Up
in Crosswords

Crossword Mysteries by Nero Blanc

THE CROSSWORD MURDER
TWO DOWN
THE CROSSWORD CONNECTION
A CROSSWORD TO DIE FOR
A CROSSWORDER'S HOLIDAY
CORPUS DE CROSSWORD
A CROSSWORDER'S GIFT
ANATOMY OF A CROSSWORD
WRAPPED UP IN CROSSWORDS

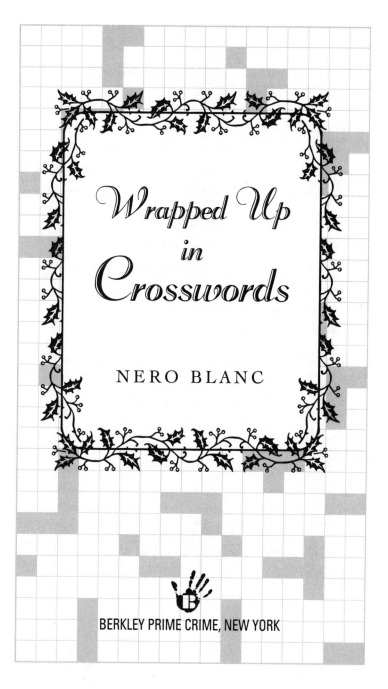

Wrapped Up
in
Crosswords

NERO BLANC

BERKLEY PRIME CRIME, NEW YORK

THE BERKLEY PUBLISHING GROUP
Published by the Penguin Group
Penguin Group (USA) Inc.
375 Hudson Street, New York, New York 10014, USA
Penguin Group (Canada), 10 Alcorn Avenue, Toronto, Ontario M4V 3B2, Canada
(a division of Pearson Penguin Canada Inc.)
Penguin Books Ltd., 80 Strand, London WC2R 0RL, England
Penguin Group Ireland, 25 St. Stephen's Green, Dublin 2, Ireland (a division of Penguin Books
Ltd.)
Penguin Group (Australia), 250 Camberwell Road, Camberwell, Victoria 3124, Australia
(a division of Pearson Australia Group Pty. Ltd.)
Penguin Books India Pvt. Ltd., 11 Community Centre, Panchsheel Park, New Delhi—110 017, India
Penguin Group (NZ), Cnr. Airborne and Rosedale Roads, Albany, Auckland 1310, New Zealand
(a division of Pearson New Zealand Ltd.)
Penguin Books (South Africa) (Pty.) Ltd., 24 Sturdee Avenue, Rosebank, Johannesburg 2196, South
Africa

Penguin Books Ltd., Registered Offices: 80 Strand, London WC2R 0RL, England

This book is an original publication of The Berkley Publishing Group.

This is a work of fiction. Names, characters, places, and incidents either are the product of the author's imagination or are used fictitiously, and any resemblance to actual persons, living or dead, business establishments, events, or locales is entirely coincidental.

First edition: 0-425-19974-6

Library of Congress Cataloging-in-Publication Data

Blanc, Nero.
    Wrapped up in crosswords / Nero Blanc.
        p. cm.
    ISBN 0-425-19974-6
    1. Graham, Belle (Fictitious character)—Fiction. 2. Polycrates, Rosco (Fictitious character)—
    Fiction. 3. Private investigators—Massachusetts—Fiction. 4. Crossword puzzle makers—
    Fiction. 5. Fugitives from justice—Fiction. 6. Crossword puzzles—Fiction. 7. Married people—
    Fiction. 8. Massachusetts—Fiction. 9. Dogs—Fiction. I. Title

PS3552.L365W73 2004
813'.54—dc22   2004049025

printed in the united states of america

10   9   8   7   6   5   4   3   2   1

A Letter from Nero Blanc

Dear Friends,

We were inspired to write this story because we have been blessed to share our home and life with a number of avian and canine friends. All of them have participated in our literary activities: a parakeet who was fond of typing (the m and virgule were her specialty), a parakeet who liked to wrestle with folded sheets of paper, a dog who recognized the novelist's groans of frustration as pleas for the wet nose of solace and compassion, a dog who knew the importance of leaving work behind in favor of a rejuvenating walk . . .

If our animal friends were able to *effectively* use the keyboard, this is the story they might have dreamed up. We hope you have as much fun reading it as we did creating it; and as always, we invite your comments and thoughts through our web site: www.CrosswordMysteries.com.

In closing, heartfelt thanks to all those kind and good people who work at animal shelters. Kudos!

Nero (aka Cordelia and Steve)

The authors dedicate a percentage of their earnings from *Wrapped Up in Crosswords* to The Pennsylvania Society for the Prevention of Cruelty to Animals*

* The Pennsylvania Society for the Prevention of Cruelty to Animals (PSPCA) has six rural Pennsylvania branches, in addition to its Philadelphia main office/shelter at 350 E. Erie Avenue, Philadelphia, PA 19134 - www.pspca.org.

One

OSCO Polycrates entered the Newcastle Police station through the side door on Cabot Alley. Although he'd been a private investigator for over six years, Rosco had served with the police department of this Massachusetts coastal city for eight years prior to that; and in all those fourteen years, the department had yet to alter the security entry code on the station house side door—02740. It was actually the local zip code, but it was surprising how many of the employees had trouble remembering it. Rosco had often considered suggesting to his former partner, Lieutenant Al Lever—now chief of homicide—that a numerical change might be advisable and even timely, but in the end, Rosco always nixed the notion. It was often beneficial being the only nondepartmental individual privy to this "secret" number. At the ripe old age of thirty-eight, he regarded the entry code as a "retirement bonus" unwittingly bestowed upon him by the NPD.

One of the major advantages of using the side door was that he could avoid going through the metal detector and then facing undue harassment by the desk sergeant. Having been a former officer, Rosco's stature within the Newcastle Police Department ran about 50–50; that is to say, half of the officers admired and respected him for his sense of honor and humor as well as his seemingly unorthodox, albeit efficient, approach to crime solving. The other half of the Newcastle Police Department disliked him for basically the same reasons.

On this cold but unusually snow-free morning, the twentieth of December, Rosco had even more reason for using the department's side door. Walking beside him, as he approached the building, was the latest addition to his small family: a thirty pound silver-gray bundle of canine fluff named Gabby. Just as Rosco habitually eschewed socks—except athletic ones for his morning runs—Gabby saw no use whatsoever for a leash.

The puppy had been "adopted" earlier in the year when Rosco and his wife, Annabella Graham, had been in Los Angeles. "Belle," as she was known to friends and fans, was the crossword puzzle editor for *The Evening Crier,* one of Newcastle's two daily papers. She was also—although it made Rosco more than a little anxious—an amateur sleuth, and had been called to L.A. as technical consultant for a TV movie based on one of her more prominent cases. After some unpleasant business involving the murder of the show's screenwriter, Belle and Rosco had been left with the door prize, which was Gabby.

Belle liked to describe the puppy as a cross between a miniature poodle and a wheaten *terrorist;* at this point it was difficult to tell whether Gabby was more besotted with Rosco or vice versa. The two had become inseparable. When Rosco left their house on Captain's Walk without her, she either spent the day sulking or demanding attention from her "sister," Kit. When Rosco returned home, Gabby flew into such an ecstasy that Kit, who was a shepherd mix and older and wiser by a full year, would turn away in disgust. Then she'd seek out Belle, leaning her large body against her as though in empathy.

Needless to say, this adoring act brought results with Rosco. He found excuses to take Gabby on many excursions, and since his "mission" today was not of a crime-solving nature, he saw no reason why the newest member of the household shouldn't accompany him. The likelihood of any desk sergeant allowing him to enter the police station with a dog seemed remote, which was another solid reason to cherish his possession of the entry code for the Cabot Alley door.

Before Rosco had left the Newcastle Police Department, he, Al Lever, and forensics wizard, Abe Jones, had taken it upon themselves to organize a holiday toy drive for the city's neediest children. The initial effort had grown, and the three men now collected close to three hundred gifts—which they and a group of stalwart friends then wrapped and redistributed to Newcastle's several homeless shelters, its two social services agencies, a host of after-school programs that aided kids at risk, and the hospital's pediatric ward. The bounty was delivered Christmas day in time for each institution's annual party.

Although Rosco was no longer with the department, he wouldn't have given up involvement with the gift drive for the world. And this was his "mission" on this particular Tuesday: to team up with Jones and Lever, don holiday costumes, and retrieve gifts the local merchants had been gathering from their customers since Thanksgiving.

As Rosco and his dog stepped onto the olive-green linoleum of the station house's inner hallway, the heavy metal exit door slammed behind them with a crash. Gabby leapt six inches in the air at the sudden noise, then turned toward the offensive slab of black steel and yipped three times in rapid and noisy succession. Neither her barking nor the clang of the door seemed to garner the attention of any of the officers, most of whom were too involved in their own particular pieces of police business. Rosco acknowledged the nod of a plainclothes officer as he passed. The man was escorting a known drug dealer down the hallway, the detainee's handcuffs being the only item that distinguished cop from hoodlum. Gabby gave both a low growl as they ambled by, and the cop laughed.

"And a Merry Christmas to you, too, pooch. You better teach her who the good guys are, Rosco, before she runs off with the likes of Archie, here."

"We're working on that. Her previous housemate was arrested on murder-one, so this is sort of a work-release program Belle and I have going. Gab's a parolee."

The cop laughed again and continued down to the stairway that led to "lock-up," or "the hole," depending on which officer you spoke to.

Rosco scanned the inner action of the NPD. Not only hadn't the security code at the side door been changed in fourteen years, nothing else appeared to have been altered either. Most of the cops were the same ones he knew from his stint there. There were a couple of new faces, but not many; and the walls had probably been painted a few times, but their color was the same institutional green it had always been. *Does the city get a deal on this paint?* Rosco wondered. Dusty ceiling fans hung down and rotated lazily, even in late December. The idea was to move the heat, coffee fumes, and cigarette smoke around so that no one felt slighted. Rosco guessed that NO SMOKING signs at NPD were still a good five years off.

The large room, separated into fifteen work cubicles, was

sparsely populated. Only five or six officers worked quietly, filling out paperwork, while two groups of uniformed patrol-men and -women swapped jokes at two separate coffee stations on either side of the duty desk. A feeble attempt had been made to give the place a touch of holiday cheer. The desk sergeant, who had her back to Rosco, wore reindeer antlers instead of a police hat, and a string of red and green lights had been hung along the back wall—the same string of lights Rosco had purchased eight years ago. About twenty percent of the bulbs had blown out and had yet to be re-placed.

On the far side of the room were three glass-paneled of-fices. An artificial wreath hung on the door closest to the duty desk. It belonged to the captain. Rosco was relieved to see the office empty, the captain being one of the officers with whom Rosco had often been at odds. The center office belonged to the captain's executive officer. It was empty as well. And the final room belonged to Rosco's ex-partner, Al Lever. Al could be seen perched behind his desk, his back to the station house, reading the *Crier* and smoking a cigarette.

Rosco looked down at Gabby and said, "I see that our friend Detective Lever has finally kicked that nasty habit of chewing nicotine gum all day long."

Gabby let out a small whine. Her previous housemate, as Rosco had referred to her, had found great success using "the patch," but Gabby had no effective means of communicating this information to either Rosco or Al.

As Rosco worked his way across the station house, with Gabby at his heels, his progress was slowed as "The Gabs," or "The Gabsters," or "Gabby-Girl" received pats and treats from Rosco's old pals, and disapproving scowls from his for-mer detractors. When they reached the lieutenant's door, Rosco tapped twice on the glass and walked in.

Lever swiveled in his chair, glanced at his watch, and dropped the newspaper on his desk, along with a chewed No. 2 pencil. He'd clearly been working the daily crossword puzzle. He stubbed out his cigarette and intentionally gave Rosco's surname the same drawn-out and inaccurate pronunciation he'd been giving it for years and years. What had started out as an off-hand reference to Rosco's Greek heritage had become a familiar and collegial habit—an inside joke between two old friends.

"Poly—crates. What's up? Ten o'clock already, huh?"

Rosco glanced down at the puzzle. "Yep. Time sure flies when you're wrapped up in serious investigative police work."

His former partner was only a year or two older than Rosco, but those years had left their mark. Where Rosco was fit, with thick, dark hair and a lean, youthful face, Al Lever was overweight, balding, pasty white, and had a constant smoker's cough—even on those rare occasions when he'd switched from cigarettes to nicotine gum. And he loved to play the curmudgeon: the gruff, hardboiled cop who had little time for chit-chat and life's small pleasantries.

Al tapped the newspaper. "This is all the fault of that wife of yours. If she hadn't gotten me hooked on crosswords, a hell of lot more work would get done around here."

Rosco laughed. "Hey Al, what are friends for? You want me to take a peek at the answers for you, you have only to say the word—as it were. I know where Belle stashes her unpublished work, and I'm certainly not above bribes. My hockey skates are looking a little ratty."

Lever cocked his head to one side. "Hmm . . . There's an excellent idea. And I pay my snitches well." He lit another cigarette, tossed the match into an overflowing ashtray, then pushed the crossword aside and sighed heavily. "I was hoping

Belle's puzzle here would give me some inspiration—all that clever info she tosses in: vintage movies and rare birds and quotations and things . . . 'cause I've been wracking my brains for a Christmas gift for my wife—"

"Surprise, surprise, what else is new?"

Lever scowled. "I take it you've got your honey's present already covered in shiny paper and hidden away, is that it?"

"Well, no . . ."

"So, let's not throw stones in glass houses, shall we?"

Rosco laughed. "No pretty package for Helen to open, huh?"

"No, but I think you just supplied the solution . . . You sneak me the answers to Belle's holiday puzzle contest for the *Crier,* I score the newspaper's prize of 'a deluxe dinner for two,' and *bingo,* I've got a nice I.O.U. to lay on my wife on Christmas morning . . . Then I take the little lady out to dine the minute the winner's announced on New Year's Eve. Problem solved . . . I like it, buddy. I say, let's go for it."

"Except that it's kinda illegal to rig a competition."

"Yeah, I know . . ." Lever made a sound that was less a chortle than a groan. "So, what are you getting Belle?"

This time it was Rosco's turn to sigh. "Not a clue."

Al returned to the puzzle and filled in a word. "A partridge in a pear tree . . . How's about that?"

"This is no joking matter. I'm running out of time here."

"It wasn't a joke. I like pears. Give her an I.O.U. for that fancy nursery up the coast aways, cut out a photo of a cute, little bird. In fact, maybe that's not a bad notion for me to consider" . . .

At this point, Gabby interrupted the conversation by jumping up, placing her front paws on Lever's desk, and attempting to grab what was left of a jelly doughnut.

"Hey, hey," Al barked. "This is a police station, in case you two haven't noticed." He glowered at Gabby as though spying her for the first time. "How'd you get that mutt past O'Hara at the duty desk?"

"You know O'Hara; she's never been very observant."

"Didn't anyone tell you there's a leash law in this city?"

Rosco gently lifted Gabby's paws from the desk and placed them back on the floor. "Bad girl."

"That didn't have a very authoritative ring to it, Polycrates. That's the most spoiled dog in Newcastle. If I pull your name at our Secret Santa party, I'm getting you, both of you, a leash."

Gabby dropped her head and walked behind Rosco as Al continued, "And then I'm assigning a patrolman to follow you around town, just to be sure you use the dang thing."

Lever's office door opened once more and Abe Jones walked in.

"What is this?" Al grumbled. "No one knocks around here?"

"Hey, Al, you're talking to Rosco; how important could it be? And besides, we're meeting at ten, right?" Jones shook Rosco's hand and looked down at his feet, spotting Gabby. He dropped into a crouch and held his arms open. "Well if it ain't the Gabsters. How's my second-favorite canine?"

Gabby placed her paws on Abe's thighs and began licking his face.

"Arrgh," Lever growled. "You two and your dogs; you're making me sick. I'm gonna puke, really."

"Kiss the girls and make them cry," Jones said as he straightened. He was younger and slightly taller than Rosco, African-American, and in perfect physical shape. He looked like a movie star masquerading as a forensics expert. "So, are we ready to do this thing?"

Lever stood. "Yep."

"I take it the costumes are still up in the evidence room?" Rosco asked. "Or is that the one thing that's changed since the last time I was here?"

Jones laughed. "Nothing changes, Rosco. Nothing ever changes."

"Ho, ho." Lever pointed at Gabby. "What are you going to do with the dog while we're up there?"

"The dog?" Rosco asked incredulously.

"The dog."

Rosco shrugged. "She can't come with us? She's very well behaved."

Jones suppressed a laugh, and Gabby gave him a dirty look.

"No dogs in the evidence room," Lever announced.

"Come on, Al . . ."

"No dogs in the evidence room."

"Who's gonna know besides us?"

"No dogs in the evidence room."

"Come on, lighten up, Al, it's Christmas," Abe said.

"Not for five more days it isn't. No dogs in the evidence room. How many times do I have to say it?"

Rosco shook his head. "Man, talk about a Scrooge. If we leave her in your office, Al, I guarantee you won't have any doughnuts left when we get back. Even if you stick them all the way on top of the filing cabinets in the corner." He patted Gabby's head. "Besides, look at that face. How can you say 'no' to that?"

"You two make me sick."

"Me and Abe?"

"All *three* of you . . ." Lever let out a lengthy and very stagy sigh, sat on the edge of his desk, and folded his arms over his chest. "Okay, just this once. But keep an eye on her. You know the penalty for destroying evidence?"

"Ten years in the pound?"

Two

osco, Abe Jones, and Al Lever meandered up the flight of stairs leading to the second floor of the Newcastle Police Department. Gabby ran ahead, which was a major part of her personality. She saw no point in walking if she could do the one-hundred-yard dash instead.

The top floor of the building consisted of two large rooms set on either end of a long, cheerless hallway. Both sides of the corridor held four sets of doors. The smaller spaces behind the doors were soundproof and flexible in nature, being either connected by two-way mirrors and used for questioning detainees, or available for confidential meetings or temporary office space. The same dingy, green paint that made the first floor so eye-catching and delightful covered the upstairs walls, but here the linoleum covering the floor was a dark and grubby gray that hadn't seen industrial-strength cleaner or a buffing machine in ages. In the dim fluorescent lighting, the corridor looked like a mine shaft. The evidence room sat at the far end, and as soon as the three men caught up to Gabby at the top of the stairs, she ran down the hall and waited in front of the door.

"See, Al?" Rosco said with a laugh, and a touch of pride. "See how smart she is? She knew exactly where we were going."

"Yeah, right. There's probably an old leg of lamb in there. One that someone once used as a murder weapon, no doubt. I know how dogs think. Chow. And that's about it."

Rosco pointed to Al's sizable belly. "You know of which you speak."

"*Harumph* . . . You'll never catch me with a dog again, I'll tell you that much."

"What dog would want you?" Abe chortled. "I'm surprised your wife sticks around with the amount of cigarette smoke you generate."

"Me?" All grumbled. "You're one to talk. You can't even *find* a wife. Every time I see you, you're with a different woman."

Abe laughed again and placed his arm over Lever's shoulder. "I've *found* plenty of wives, Al, just none I care to marry."

"Ho, ho."

"This 'ho ho' appears to be Al's new laugh, cooked up especially for the holiday season," Rosco said to Jones with a raised eyebrow. "Who said he was a Scrooge . . . ? Not very original, but better than Bah, Humbug."

"Keep it up, you two. Keep it up."

They reached the door to the evidence room where Gabby was waiting, her short tail wagging in anticipation of what treats might lie on the other side. Al pulled a bundle of keys from his pocket, unlocked and opened the broad steel door, then flipped on the light switch. The same fluorescent lighting that illuminated the remainder of the building flickered a few times before settling into a garish, pale green glow. An alarm panel on the wall next to the door emitted a steady tone until Al punched a five-number entry code on a keypad. Unlike the building's central code, this was a closely guarded NPD secret, the numbers changed regularly and released to only a select few. No police officer liked to have evidence tampered with.

The room was simple in design: a thirty-by-forty-foot storage area with twelve metal shelving units that stretched from floor to ceiling and ran the length of the room. Each of them was chockablock with crime scene evidence, the items stored in clear plastic bags that had been heat-sealed and affixed with tags listing contents, case number, and officers assigned. Gabby ran down one of the aisles as soon as the alarm tone ended.

"Keep an eye on that mutt, Rosco," Lever groused.

"Everything's sealed, Al. There's nothing she can get into."

Jones resisted saying *Famous last words,* as the three men walked over to the fifth aisle and strolled halfway down. Atop the highest shelf sat a number of large cardboard boxes, each of which had originally held a case of paper towels. The current contents were the only items in the room not sealed in plastic, and they'd been labeled with a black marking pen: Santas, Wise Men, Musketeers, and Mice.

"What'd we dress up as last year?" Lever said, almost to himself.

Abe and Rosco grumbled "Three Blind Mice" in unison. They made no attempt to mask their lack of enthusiasm for the outfits.

"Right. Personally, I think we looked kind of foolish in those getups."

"Foolish?" Rosco said facetiously. "Nahhh . . ."

"They were your idea, Al," Abe pointed out. "If I never

dress up as a mouse again, I'll be a happy man. I vote for the Santas. Everyone likes them."

"Santas, it is." Lever retrieved two boxes and he and Rosco carried them to the end of the aisle. Inside were three complete costumes: red plush suits, white beards, curly wigs, black boots, and two down pillows. The activity of the men had attracted Gabby's attention, and she came barreling up the next aisle with a plastic bag between her teeth. It contained a pair of loafers caked in dry mud.

Lever sighed deeply. "Put them back, Rosco."

"Bad girl, Gab," Rosco said as he removed the bag from her mouth. "Where'd you get this from?"

"Just put them back. There's a file number on the tag. You don't need to have a conversation about it. The dog can't understand you."

"That's what you think."

"I swear, Poly-crates, sometimes I really wonder about you." Lever sighed again; then he and Jones slipped out of their street clothes and began putting on the Santa costumes.

"*Arrgh,* these must be Rosco's trousers," Al said as he attempted to fasten the waist hook of his outfit.

"What's the tag say?"

"Well, the tag says, 'Al,' but they must have gotten mixed up somehow."

Abe laughed, held up the remaining pair of red pants, and read the tag. "Nope. These say, 'Rosco.' And even taking into consideration that Polycrates and I need to use 'fat' pillows, there's no way you're getting into these pants. Methinks you've gained a few pounds, my friend."

"Let me see those." Lever grabbed the trousers from Jones as Rosco and Gabby returned from replacing the evidence bag.

"No, those are mine, Al," Rosco said. "See, there's a P on the waistband right next to the hook. Yours has an L."

"Yep," Abe said, "mine has a J. Sorry, Al, better suck it in."

Lever tried once more to button the trousers. "Maybe we should go as the Wise Men instead?"

"Forget it." Jones stepped in front of the lieutenant. "We did Wise Men two years ago. Remember, we kept tripping all over those long robes? And Rosco insisted on firing up the frankincense? It smelled worse than your cigarettes. We're sticking with Santas." He grabbed Lever's waistband on either side. "Okay, Al, on three. One . . . two . . . three . . . Suck it in."

Lever pulled in his stomach, and Jones fastened the hook. "There you go, nothing to it."

Lever groaned. "I feel like a stuffed sausage."

"No comment," Rosco said.

"Besides, Santa's supposed to be overweight," Abe offered.

"Don't get on me with the 'overweight' business, Abe."

"I said 'Santa,' not you, Al. Although, maybe a few sessions at the gym—"

"Forget it, Jones. You know what you can do with that exercise advice of yours. Besides, if the Good Lord wanted me to look like you, he wouldn't have invented jelly doughnuts. Now let's get going before I split these duds apart. We've got some toys to collect."

THE first stop on their route was Hatch's Hardware Store. It was owned and operated by Stanley Hatch, who at fifty-four still found himself occasionally referred to as "Old Mr. Hatch's grandson." The shop had been a Newcastle institution for well over a hundred years, and like many of the city's landmarks, it looked nearly the same as it had the day it opened its doors for business: a pair of cluttered display windows bracketing a covered entry that was paved with beige tiles into which the name 'S. Hatch & Sons' was imprinted in scrolling black.

On the sidewalk fronting the entrance were wooden barrels crammed with snow shovels and thick-bristled brooms, while both sides of the doorway were piled with sacks of rock-salt and a pyramid of blue plastic bottles containing windshield deicer. Inside, the store was deep and wide, its age-darkened walls covered with oak shelving that reached the full fifteen feet to the ceiling. Antiquated rolling ladders allowed Stanley and his minions to access merchandise that lay out of reach, while the remainder was stacked on dusty shelves that ran lengthwise down the center aisles. To say the place appeared crowded and old-fashioned would have been an understatement. Hatch's gave the impression that you could find horse-pulled plows or barrels of whale oil if you only knew where to look—and maybe you could have.

The flooring was also oak, wide-planked and redolent with decades of floor oil and shoe leather. Gabby loved the smell; she also enjoyed pestering Ace, Stanley's aging collie who was such a fixture in the shop that clerks and customers alike instinctively stepped around his snoozing form. When the three Santas entered Hatch's, Gabby trotted off in search of the collie while Abe Jones turned to regard Lever and the cigarette that dangled between his frizzy, synthetic beard and mustache. "Are you sure you can smoke in here, Al?"

"The day you can't smoke in a hardware store will be the day—"

"You quit?"

"Ho, ho."

"Just be careful you don't set yourself on fire, okay?"

Rosco pointed to a bright red fire extinguisher. "If he's going to torch himself, this is the place to do it." He picked up the device and mimed hooking it onto Al's wide black belt.

"There you go. It even matches your trousseau; Albert, you look de-vine."

"Let me guess who we have here," Stanley Hatch said as he approached the visitors. He was tall and angular with an engaging smile and kind eyes set in a long and thoughtful face. Although there was nothing broad-shouldered or he-man-outdoorsy about him, he was the kind a guy who could repair just about anything and do it well. He also had a self-effacing air and a quiet humor that sat well with both new customers and longtime friends. "Oddly enough, you resemble a certain trio of blind rodents that appeared last year around this time." Stan's tone was jocular, and it nearly disguised the touch of sadness that colored his words; his wife had died eighteen months before, and his grief at losing her hadn't wholly diminished. "I think I prefer the smoking Santa to the smoking rat," he added in an attempt to brighten the mood.

"It was a mouse, Stan," rejoined Lever with an unusually gentle smile.

"Al, I supply all sorts of traps around here: large, small, have-a-hearts, raccoon cages . . . and I'm telling you, if you were supposed to be dressed up as a mouse, I wouldn't have wanted to see the rat." Then he pointed to a large wooden barrel near one the store's twin display windows. It was over-filled with toys: footballs, dolls, and stuffed animals of all shapes and sizes. "Pretty good haul this year," he said with pride. "Folks have been really generous . . ." He walked over to the center aisle, removed three boxed coffee makers from a shelf and handed them to Rosco. "Something for the parents."

"Thanks, Stan. Well, we'd better load up and be on our way. Remember, our annual wrapping and supper party is on the twenty-third. Try to make it if you can. Sara Briephs is hosting this year, and you know the kind of spread she puts out."

"I'll see." The smile was pensive.

"It'll do you good."

Stan nodded and brightened his smile. "I'm sure it would."

"Besides, we need all the help we can get," Rosco continued. "Last year's haul hit five hundred items."

Stan nodded again. He seemed about to speak, then opted for silence.

"Sara would love to have you."

"She's a grand old lady," Stanley said in answer. "The city wouldn't be the same without her." He paused, then concluded with a simple "Thanks." And that single word conveyed every emotion the group needed.

"Hey, what's a Santa for?" was Al response.

It took the threesome several trips to get the gifts packed into their unmarked police van. When they'd finished, Rosco whistled for Gabby, and the quartet marched down the street toward their next stop, Robertson's Stationery Supply. But as they passed the pet shop window, Al stopped and pointed. "There you go, Rosco. There's your gift for Belle—a live partridge for that pear tree I suggested."

Rosco, Abe, and Gabby had already reached the jewelry store on the corner. They turned and rejoined Lever.

"Those are lovebirds, Al. Not partridges," Jones pointed out.

"Birds schmirds. It's the thought that counts. You guys have no Christmas spirit. And women love birds. Lovebirds; get it? Come on, Rosco, look at how cute that one on the left is—"

"You don't just buy one of them, Al. They're a pair. They come in a pair."

"A pair in a pear tree," was the laconic reply. "I like it."

"Actually . . ." Rosco said. They could see the wheels beginning to turn in his head as he fiddled with the tips of his snow-white mustache. "Actually, you've given me an idea. There's a slight logistical problem, though . . ."

"So? What's your plan?" Jones asked.

"Are you nuts? Like I'm going to tell you guys! I might as well put it on the eleven o'clock news."

"Come on, Rosco, how are you going to sneak a pair of—" Lever was interrupted by the ringing of his cell phone. He removed his bulky Santa gloves, lifted the phone from his belt, and glanced at the caller I.D. readout. "Duty calls." He brought it to his ear and said, "Lieutenant Lever."

After about thirty seconds Al tapped a button on the phone and clipped it back on his belt. "We're going to have to pack it in, boys. The captain's called an emergency briefing, and I need to head back with the van. All personnel—so I guess that means you, too, Abe. Rosco, you'd better beam in with the rest of the merchants and tell them we'll be around tomorrow. Unless you want to continue solo."

"What's up?"

"Three inmates just broke out of the Suffolk County Jail in Boston. State police believe they may be heading south."

Three

GABBY barreled up the narrow staircase of the quaint late-eighteenth-century house in Newcastle's historic Captain's Walk. As was the puppy's wont, she flew up over the steps two at a time, then roared around the landing's uncarpeted corner, bolted down the hall, slid through Belle and Rosco's bedroom door, and made a spectacular leap to land squarely in the center of the quilt upon which Kit, the senior canine resident of the Graham-Polycrates household, had been peacefully snoozing. Gabby's short barks, yips, and yowls could only be translated as "Wake up! Wake up! Wake up!"

The noise was anxious and overwrought, but then Gabby enjoyed creating caverns out of tooth-sized cavities. When the mailman came to the door—which as everyone knew was a daily occurrence—she behaved as though the house were being stormed by brigands. Kit, on the other hand, was beyond such shenanigans; running around inside was the type of childish activity she'd outgrown the moment this little gray monster moved in. She was now far too refined to leave rumpled carpets in her wake or fly off the handle at every noise. After all, her mother was a pure-bred German shepherd with papers to prove it, and her father was . . . was . . . Okay, so nobody's perfect. He might have been part beagle.

"Wake up!" Gabby yipped again. She bounced up and down, another habit Kit found profoundly annoying.

Kit sighed, opened one eye, and twitched a sleepy white paw. Gabby's exuberance was putting a damper on a perfectly good and well-deserved nap.

"Wake up, you lazy . . . dog!" The dog was added as a slur that almost sounded like a yelp of pain.

Kit merely stretched her brown, white, and black sixty-pound body across the toasty quilt, exposing the pale speckled fur of her belly. She didn't bother to point out the obvious: that Gabby was also a dog, and could well be accused of laxity when it came to issues involving toil—such as the all-important task of taking the two human members of the clan for their daily perambulation. Kit was too much of a lady to stoop to such discourtesy.

"Wake up! Wake up! Wake up!"

This is getting old. Kit sighed again. *Terriers,* she thought, *even part terriers, were bossy creatures.* Kit half-raised her head, staring at her nervous companion with dark and placid eyes. "Mmmm?" escaped from her throat. The sound was open to interpretation, but Kit was attempting patience.

"Okay, okay, okay. Here's the deal. Rosco's making a crossword puzzle!" Gabby spouted in a succession of staccato yaps. "And he's doing it on the Q.T.! I caught him sneaking a peek at Belle's reference books while she was down in the cellar pulling stuff out of the clothes drier. He's mumbling to himself, like he does when he's working on something real confusing; like that case out on Cape Cod when we all went to the beach and he muttered stupid stuff all the time—"

Kit thought it better not to correct Gabby's egregious grammar at this moment; instead, she interrupted with another low-keyed "Mmmm?"

"So, that's real bad, right? I mean, like, really, *really* bad, and suspicious, too. 'Cause everyone knows Rosco doesn't make crosswords. Belle does."

Kit produced a third "Mmmm . . ."

"Do you want to hear this story or not?" Gabby didn't wait for a reply; instead, she raced ahead with her tale, rapidly kneading her two front paws on the downy coverlet as she chattered away. In Kit's estimation, the long curly hair spreading out around the claws made Gabby's feet resemble dirty dust mops. Kit's own, of course, were a snowy white, and she kept them meticulously clean.

"And what do you think I heard him writing?"

Again, Kit deemed it advisable not to correct this error. Writing was intended to be "seen" rather than "heard," but Gabby had not had Kit's youthful advantages: a former university professor as a companion to her earliest puppyhood, then a transfer to this home which was inhabited by a master wordsmith, a female human who loved to read dictionary and encyclopedia entries aloud. Gabby would learn syntax and a more exacting vocabulary eventually—that is, if she ever remained quiet enough to listen to her elders and betters.

" 'I owe you one pair of love.' That's what I heard Rosco say. 'I owe you one pair of love.' And you know what that means, don't you? Don't you?"

Kit didn't answer. Gabby was still a youngster. Why spoil her little game?

"It means Rosco's getting that disgusting pair of lovebirds I saw in the shop window this morning, that's what! Lovebirds as a surprise Christmas present for Belle! Birds in this house, Kit! Birds! Do you know how awful that will be?"

"Are you sure you're not barking up the wrong tree? Maybe Rosco's taking Al's advice about the pear—"

"No, he's not! No, he's not! No, he's not . . . ! Look, we were walking down the street, all four of us—this is before Al got the call about the cons—when the humans came to a sudden stop . . . You know, like they do when something startles them? Anyway, Rosco started staring hard at the window." Gabby in her anxiety hopped up and down on the bed while Kit's velvet-soft ears quivered under the loud assault of the terrier voice. "He was studying this stupid pair of birds. And now he's making a puzzle about them."

"It could be a pair of anything, Gabby. Socks, for instance." Kit had a great fondness for the athletic socks Rosco used for running. Stuffed with newspapers, they had been among her earliest toys. That is, until the humans had realized she preferred the clean ones stored in the bureau drawer. "Or shoes."

"Don't be stupid. Socks aren't lovely—"

"Shoes are. Some especially so. Belle had a glorious pair of red pumps that I found delightful to chew . . . one anyway. Too much of the same leathers and dyes can be off-putting to the taste buds. That's why I only nibble a single shoe of a set. Or did, I should say, before—"

"You dumb dog! Nobody writes an I.O.U. for shoes—or socks—and puts it in a crossword puzzle! Who'd bother with all that work? You might as well say: I owe you a pair of mittens, for Pete's sake. Or pajamas. Or pants. Something mundane like that. Anyway, I lived in California, remember? You've never even been there, so you don't have a clue. But I do. I know a lot about pet birds . . . parrots . . . cockatiels . . . macaws . . . mynahs . . . They were real popular there, and boy, are they a noisy bunch! And talk about a mess! Seeds, poop . . . All they do is squawk. And you can bet Rosco won't keep them in their cage where they belong, and—" Gabby, in her frenzy, failed to see that Kit was growing dangerously impatient with her antics. Not to mention, the amount of terrier "noise."

" 'Dumb' for your information, my dear young Gabby, means 'devoid of the power of speech'—which I am not." The 'my dear' was not expressed as an affectionate purr, but Gabby also failed to notice this fact.

"You are so! You're a dumb dog, Kit!"

"I am most certainly not dumb!"

"Are, too!"

"I am not!'

"Are too! Are too! Are too!"

"No!!!!" This was expressed as a full-fledged growl, and it unfortunately coincided with Belle's entry into the room. In her hands was a wicker basket filled with clean laundry. The static electricity produced by all those freshly folded clothes made her blue pullover sweater appear to ripple and swell in size, and her fine, pale blonde hair to wave Medusa-like in the air. If the two residents of the bed hadn't known her better, Belle would have seemed a formidable sight indeed.

She plopped the basket on the bed and ran distracted fingers through her hair while her gray eyes leveled on Kit and Gabby with an expression of mock severity. "All this yipping and yapping . . . What are you girls doing? I could hear you all the way down in the cellar. And you, Kitty. Growling at poor, little Gab. Shame on you."

"Kitty" gave Belle a lofty glance, then crossed her front paws with careful grace while Gabby burrowed into the concealing folds of down, hiding her head.

"Shameless," Kit grumbled.

"I'm not getting off this bed! I'm not getting off this bed!

I'm not! I'm not!" Gabby retorted, but the sound to Belle's ears was more whimper than defiance.

"Awww, Gab, sweetheart," Belle said as she began stroking the puppy's curling coat. "Kit didn't mean to be unkind. Did you, Kitty? There's room for both of you. Isn't there? Move over now, and let Gab have a little more space."

Of course, both "girls" understood every word of this directive, although Kit's native tongue was Massachusetts Mutt and Gabby's California Canine. It was Belle and Rosco who were the least linguistically facile of the four residents of the house. They were familiar with only human discourse. But then, they could open the refrigerator door, and that was an ability highly prized by those who could not.

Kit rolled onto her other side in apparent acquiescence, then crossed her front paws once more.

"Okay, you two. No more fighting. As soon as I put the laundry away, Rosco and I are going to take you to the dog park to see your buddies. You both need to run off some steam."

Kit sighed at Belle's naïveté; every canine knew that "walks" and "visits to the dog park" were intended as diversions for humans, not dogs. But then the poor two-legged things simply stood around talking rather than taking advantage of the wonders nature held in store.

"I'm not letting any darn birds into this house," Gabby groused while Belle proceeded with her task and Kit turned her attention to Rosco's rolled running socks which were stowed in a drawer well out of her four-legged reach.

"Watch your mouth, Gabby," Kit murmured, mesmerized by the sight of those round white balls which fit so easily between the teeth and are so pleasant to munch upon.

"You watch yours," Gabby sneered back.

"Don't be flippant with me, young lady."

Four

NEWS of Rosco's surreptitious crossword and his ill-conceived plan to introduce avian life into his happy home raced around the park and among the four-legged members of "the canine corps" as dire news often does—the yips and yowls increasing in disbelieving pain with each voiced opinion. But as far as the "corps'" human members were concerned—that being: Belle, Rosco, Abe Jones, Martha Leonetti (top-dog waitress at Lawson's Coffee Shop), and Bartholomew Kerr, the city's notorious if diminutive gossip columnist—the noises made by their four-footed friends were no more than their customary yaps and woofs and growls. But, of course, the humans were consigned to exchange their views in the most rudimentary manner: a Massachusetts version of the English language.

"You're friggin' kiddin' me," Buster lamented. He was Abe Jones' companion, a part-chocolate Lab and a tough talker who hated to be referred to as a "Lab mix," or a "Lab" anything. "I mean, jeez," he'd complain, "this guy works in a

"I'll eat them first, that's what I'll do. Birds. Yech. Those miserable little feathered—"

"Girls," Belle ordered. "Now skedaddle. If you can't get along, we'll keep you separated. And you won't be able to spend the day napping on our bed."

"*Whose* bed?" Gabby demanded, but her meaning was lost on Belle.

friggin' forensic *lab* all day long . . . You'd think he'd want to claim I was a mixture of something else: Chesapeake Bay retriever or Gordon setter or something like that."

To which Martha's saffron-gold Pekingese, Princess, would invariably respond: "Maybe because your retrieving skills are chancy, and you rarely ever *set.*" Belying her delicate—some might even say "prissy" appearance, her pouffe of a tail and silken ruff—Princess was every bit the salty-tongued original as was her two-legged friend and housemate, Ms. Leonetti.

But today, the normal quibbles and rivalries—even the compliments—were cast aside. Each canine visitor to the park, which stood on the spacious, cliffside grounds of the now-defunct Dew Drop Inn, was on high alert. Today, they'd have to let the humans perform their daily duty of standing around and gabbing with one another without any four-legged assistance. There would be no attempts to get them to toss a ball or stick or Frisbee. These people would need to invent their own form of exercise today.

"Lovebirds!" Buster yelped. "You remember the nightmare I went through when Abe's mom brought her dang parakeet for a visit? And that was just one tiny—"

"I recall that you tried to eat it," Princess stated. She was wearing a cherry-pink coat with a white faux-fur collar. She was the only one among them with a wardrobe. The others forgave her the parade of outfits—all in shades of pink that complemented Martha's Lawson's uniforms. In Princess' estimation, her stylish attire set her a cut above. She cared not a whit if the colors were inspired by a coffee shop that stubbornly clung to its late 1950s' decor.

"And I would have, too, if old Mom hadn't spotted her sweetie-pie walking around on the dining room floor. That bird would have been nothin' but a couple of green feathers dangling from yours truly's juicy lips."

There was a good deal of agreement on this point. Of course, they'd all heard Buster's story many times over, but the simple act of self-righteous revenge was always pleasant to consider.

"Man, that thing was an annoyance. Cheep, cheep, cheep, squawk, squeak. All the living day long. And when Abe's mom let the dang thing out of its cage it'd buzz me. I swear it did . . . Fly these little sorties over my ears—"

"Tell 'em about breakfast. When you were eating your kibble," Winston wheezed in his authoritative manner. He was a massive and barrel-chested English bulldog who resided with Bartholomew Kerr. "The Boss," as Kerr called Winston, was far too round for his frame, which resulted in a serious shortness of breath and the inability to run for more than a few feet at a time. He was also almost the exact opposite of Bartholomew—a man so diminutive and nearsighted as to seem almost molelike. What bound this disparate couple together were their differences: Bartholomew loved Winston's bellicose stance; "the Boss" loved Bartholomew because the guy obviously needed protection. "Old Bug-eye," Winston liked to call him.

"Yeah, so, this little bunch of lime-colored feathers starts waddling across the floor toward my chow bowl—"

"The bird was walking on the floor?" Ace interrupted as he ambled over. Although the collie was the accepted king and commander of Hatch's Hardware Store, he'd grown a trifle forgetful and hard of hearing during the eighteen months since Stanley's wife—the boon companion to his puppyhood—had died. Only very recently had Ace begun to discover some of his old *joie de vivre,* standing full-square on customers' feet and upsetting boxes of wall anchors or stove bolts with his long, resplendent tail. "Why would anyone be fool enough to allow a bird to roam the floor when a dog was present? Canines are predators, for Pete's sake. We have a rep-utation to uphold."

"Oh, Ace, don't!" Princess protested, but her mincing manner and coy tone suggested she very much admired the big dog's swagger.

"Well, we are," Ace reiterated. "That's what instinct teaches us, and you sure can't buck nature." He would have continued in this vein if Gabby hadn't interrupted.

"Then what happened? Then what happened? Then what happened?" she insisted.

"Well, I was wolfing down my chow as per usual, and I catch the little creep out of the corner of my eye. And it's walkin' toward me, instead of away. So, naturally, I let out a growl . . ."

Audible approval greeted this statement. When threat-ened with a loss of foodstuffs or even a beloved bone or chew toy, what else would you do but show serious displeasure?

". . . But the friggin' thing keeps marchin' toward me, all cocky-like with its wings puffed up as if it owned the place."

"And then what happened?" Gabby repeated in an unfa-miliar whisper.

"So, I growl at it again . . . I mean, who knows what these dopey things speak? Heads probably full of useless lyrics . . . Singing about Oklahoma or vindictive barbers, for all I know. But a growl's a growl. Even a birdbrain's gotta understand that."

"And then?" Gabby yipped.

"And then Mr. Greenie hightails it straight across the kitchen floor until its little pink feet are standing right next to my bowl, and I'm thinkin' one more step, mister, one more step . . . But then Abe's mom suddenly pops her head around the corner and spots us and sings out: 'Abe, come look, Buster's sharing his meal! What a sweet, kind, generous dog he is! There is such a thing as altruism in the animal king-dom, after all.' With that, I back up in disgust—natch; and the little thief hops up and into my friggin' chow dish and begins peckin' away . . . Ate my food!"

Noises of outrage and horror rose from the crowd. The cli-max to Buster's tale never failed to call forth primal emotions.

After his friends' reactions had died down, Buster added a take-charge: "End of story. Lesson learned: Birds belong out-side where nature put 'em. Consequence and/or projection re-garding avian affairs: We gotta' make sure the critters stay where they belong; i.e., what can we do to help you guys? One of them humans over there decides to get a little feath-ered thing that either cheeps or warbles, none of us is safe. I'm tellin' you, it's the thin end of the wedge. Maybe the hu-mans' problem is that they spend all day walkin' around on their hind legs. Or maybe it's because they don't really exer-cise. I mean, most days, Abe goes to a place he calls 'the gym', but he never comes home panting. Smells sweet as a rose, in fact. Also, these mental lapses of theirs could be due to sleep-deprivation. When have any of you see one of them take a de-cent morning nap?"

A number of grumbling "Mmmmms" greeted that assess-ment, but Buster wasn't finished. Like Abe, he liked to be thorough when presenting a case. "I've seen humans who don't eat real food, too. They munch on the kind of stuff rab-bits eat."

"Yuuucchhh! Rabbits!" the dogs spat out as a group, and the humans, still clustered on what was once the inn's rolling, ocean-view lawn, turned in worried surprise.

"They can't all be getting sick at the same time, can they?" Kit heard Belle ask.

To which Martha replied, "Well, Princess' nose was defi-nitely on the warm side this morning. I think I'd better take her home. Especially as she doesn't seem the least interested in playing today. Actually, now that I mention it, none of them do. You don't suppose some type of kennel-cough could be going around?"

With that, the two-legged friends descended on the four-legged group that had gathered near the broad steps leading up to the inn's dry-rotted and collapsing veranda. Each dog's nose was felt, and a prognosis given. Martha tucked Princess away in a special primrose-hued carrying case, climbed into her car, waved, and drove off; but the other canines—with the exception of Winston—were urged on with sticks and balls and Frisbees. The afternoon had deepened into a coppery dusk; the water spreading below the inn's quirky and multi-turreted facade was turning inky while the building itself, unlit and uninhabited, was black and sinister against the sky. It didn't look like a place anyone would have ever wanted to spend the night.

Five

$\mathcal{A}$T eight-thirty the next morning, Belle was scheduled to deliver "Belle's Nöel," this year's competition crossword to *The Evening Crier* for publication in that afternoon's *late* edition—with the winner to be announced in the *early* edition on New Year's Eve. As Al Lever and every other word-game fanatic in Newcastle knew, this was the "biggie" that "lexicographomaniacs," or folks who were crazy about crosswords, looked forward to annually—much in the same way dieters rhapsodize about hot fudge sundaes with caramelized walnuts, real whipped cream, and a side of freshly baked super-chunk chocolate chip cookies.

The prize the *Crier* offered the winning contestant was always top-notch, this year being "a deluxe dinner for two" at one of the city's new, up-market restaurants, Porto. But the chance to outdo friends and neighbors was better than a physical reward. Like any competition, the rules were strict; completed puzzles had to be returned to Belle's *Crier* office by

December 26; entrants with perfect scores were then eligible for a random drawing which took place in the office of the editor-in-chief on the morning of December 31, and involved the participation of a local bigwig—who was subsequently photographed with the lucky winner. No one in Newcastle was the least bit puzzled about the amount of attention given to a simple word game.

Before leaving home for her nominal downtown office—Belle's actual work space was the converted rear porch of the house on Captain's Walk—Rosco facetiously asked if she needed an armed guard to escort her, or handcuffs to attach her briefcase to her wrist during the short drive from their home to Newcastle's bustling commercial district. She was in the midst of straightening up her desk—a pretty futile effort—when he made the glib suggestion.

"Har har," she responded, still shuffling through notes concerning potential word play, thematic choices, and lexical references, as well as a bunch of Post-its drawn with squiggles that only she could decipher. Sometimes her own less-than-legible handwriting made the task well-nigh impossible. Belle's hands stopped moving, and she looked up at her husband. Her astute gray eyes studied him for a long minute. "You're not planning to do anything shifty are you? To help Al . . . or anyone else?"

Rosco raised two hands in the air. "Hey . . . hey . . . I wouldn't swindle my own wife. Besides, I believe that's called cheating. And cheating, as we all know—"

"Because," Belle interrupted; she knew that her husband could be very devious indeed. "Because, everyone has to be treated fairly. The puzzle doesn't appear until the *Crier*'s second edition this evening. Then correct answers have to be received by—"

"I didn't say I was up to any hanky-panky, did I?" He placed his hands tenderly on her shoulders. "Speaking of which . . ."

"You're not attempting to distract me, are you?" Belle continued to regard him. She folded her arms across her chest.

"Distract? Me? Actually, now that you mention it . . . a little distraction might be in order."

She gave him an amused smile. "How about we have a romantic dinner for two tonight? A cozy fire in the hearth . . . candles . . . a nice bottle of wine . . ."

"And me cooking?"

Belle chuckled. "Only if you want to eat something other than deviled eggs or tuna casserole—"

"Like the last tuna dish? Made with the slight omission of fish, if I recall." Rosco also laughed.

"So I forgot it, sue me. Besides, the noodles and spinach and mushrooms were tasty. Anyway, you're the culinary expert—which is one of the reasons I married you."

"I hope there was more than one reason!"

"Clause 37-A in our marriage license: The guy knows how to make real food." She gave him a long and loving kiss, then suddenly pulled away. "Darn. I forgot. Sara's coming over for supper tonight to work out the 'logistics' of the toy-wrapping party. And I promised I'd try to make a Yankee pot roast for her." Belle hunched her shoulders and smiled ruefully. " 'Try' being the operative word. I guess we'll have to postpone this tête-à-tête of ours."

Rosco looked at his wife, his arms still circling her waist. His expression was now both serious and tender. "We have our whole lives, Belle."

"Our whole lives," she repeated softly. "Aren't we lucky?"

"The luckiest people in the world."

Arm in arm, they left her office and walked through the living room to the front door. "You know, I still haven't found you a gift, Rosco. Something really special, I mean."

"You haven't?" Rosco couldn't keep the relief from his voice.

"Don't sound so pleased. I suppose you've already stashed my present in some secret corner."

"Well—"

"I wish you weren't so organized." Belle made a face. "No, I don't. What I wish is that I were more like you—never misplaced my house keys or car keys, never lost the all-important note that held the crucial clue to a puzzle: all that right-brain business you're so good at."

"But I like your left-brain qualities. Correction: I love them, and I wouldn't have you change them for the world." Rosco gave his wife another smooch. "I'll tell you what. You be my gift. You already are. Just put a nice, big, red ribbon around your waist; I'll take it from there."

"But I want you to have something wonderful to unwrap on Christmas morning."

"Didn't I just say I have you?" He stepped back and perused her from head to foot. "Maybe a gold ribbon is the way to go?"

"Mr. One-track Mind . . . So, what did you get me?"

"Would you believe me if I said I hadn't found you anything yet? Or should I say purchased, yet?"

"No." Belle looked at him. "You've hidden something right under my nose, haven't you?"

Rosco shook his head. "Scout's honor."

"Is it in the living room?" She began scanning the eclectic furnishings that offset the home's picture-perfect period restoration: a standing Victorian-era lamp with a dramatically sculpted shade, a mission-style armchair, her prized thrift-shop couch upholstered in a vintage floral fabric whose color scheme was an eye-scorching burnt orange and jungle green. "Or maybe the kitchen?

"Belle, I promise—"

At this point a prodigious amount of yipping and growling interrupted them. Kit and Gabby stood in front of the couch. Despite the amount of noise the dogs were making, there didn't appear to be any physical necessity for the argument: no questionable chew-toy ownership, no rambunctious puppy shenanigans.

"Hey, you two," Belle ordered, moving out of Rosco's embrace. "What gives?"

"Maybe it's holiday jitters," Rosco offered.

"*Hmmmphhh.* Since when do two extremely spoiled and lazy pooches worry about anything?"

"Gabby's always concerned that Kit may be getting more puppy biscuits than she is."

"My point exactly." Belle raised a wry eyebrow, then studied the dogs. "Maybe they need a little more solo time. Why don't I take Kit with me this morning?" At the sound of her name, Kit sprang forward while Gabby commenced another round of short and bossy yips. "Quiet, Gab," Belle said.

But the words fell on deaf ears, leaving Rosco to shush Gabby—which he succeeded in doing. Then he looked at his wife. "Belle," he said slowly, as she grabbed her purse, "lock your doors before you head downtown."

She cocked her head. "Expecting a serious crossword heist, are we?"

"No. It's just that . . ." Rosco paused. There was no point in frightening her, he thought. The three escaped inmates were more than likely a hundred miles away by now—if not many, many more. "The season brings out the best as well as the worst in people. I just want you to be careful, that's all."

"My middle name."

This time it was Rosco who gave her a meaningful glance. "Precisely what I mean. Caution has never been your strong suit."

"I'll make that my first New Year's resolution."

"I'm serious."

"So am I . . . sort of. Don't worry, Rosco, I'll lock my doors. No one but good-looking Greek guys dressed as Santas will be allowed a ride."

Then Belle blew him a kiss, and Gabby gave one more sharp woof. Finally, Rosco walked back to Belle's office with the vigilant dog at his heels. There, his eyes seemed to survey the room and the black and white crossword-themed decor run amok: the floor painted like a giant puzzle grid, the curtains hand-blocked with letters and numbers, the lampshades emblazoned with copies of Belle's cleverest cryptics. But, in fact, his glance didn't register any of it; instead, Rosco stood still, listening as if he expecting Belle to dart back through the front door of any moment.

When he was certain he was alone, he pulled a well-folded piece of graph paper from the rear pocket of his jeans, then he walked over to the reference books and began intently perusing the titles. "One pair of love . . ." he muttered anxiously under his breath. "I should make this rhyme somehow . . . Brings . . . Sings . . . Wings."

Gabby, however, understood each and every ominous word Rosco said. Her dark eyes had turned as hard as coal. *What rhymes with bird?* her expression said. *How about absurd? And wings? How about wrings?*

* * *

BELLE was fortunate to snag a parking space only three blocks from the venerable granite structure that housed *The Evening Crier.* As she parallel-parked—a task slightly hindered by Kit's bobbing head—she reflected on how un-Christmasy the city looked. True, the holiday decorations were all in place; beribboned wreaths and evergreen swags hung in every shop front; each streetlight was festooned with a multi-faceted metal snowflake or a jolly snowman, but what was missing was actual snow. Somehow the streets didn't feel festive without the white stuff crunching underfoot or icing the tops of shrubs or encircling the trunks of trees.

Maybe that's why I'm so tardy with my shopping this year, she thought as she and Kit climbed out of the car and began walking to the *Crier*'s offices. *I'm not in the spirit yet.* But then she reminded herself that today was December 21; it was high time she get herself in gear.

It was then that she drew to a sudden halt in front of a shop window. There, surrounded by twinkling mini-lights and giant gold bows, was the perfect gift for her husband. Chancy, yes, and definitely a splurge, but what was life for if not for taking risks? She'd already forgotten that she'd insisted that "caution" was her "middle name."

Kit, who had sauntered on ahead a couple of steps and who was now eagerly examining a bounteous display of red and green, dog and cat toys in the pet shop window, instinctively stopped at the same moment Belle did. Kit tried to follow Belle's gaze when a swirl of wings caught her quick, canine eye. There were the hateful lovebirds Gabby had described.

Kit looked up at Belle, who was still staring fixedly ahead. "I'll come back this afternoon without you in tow, Kitty," she was murmuring. "They're perfect? Don't you think? And, young lady, if you even think about eating them, you'll be in the doghouse for sure!" Kit shook herself violently, but the negative response was lost on her human companion.

ACROSS

1. Pilgrimage to Mecca
5. Mr. Dillon
9. Ms. Parks
13. Yours to Yves
14. Seafarer
15. "Once ___ a time . . ."
16. High school student
17. Christmas dessert
19. Retail items
21. Mr. Hubbard
22. Mom & ___
25. ___ Hill, D.C.
28. Chews at
29. Mallow bloom
30. Card or car man
31. That guy
32. Cancels
33. Papa Nöel
38. Bowling letters
41. N.Y. Harbor island
42. Cool
46. Tree decorations
49. "Maybe, I'll let you know."
50. Dog tethers
51. Sconces
52. Hit the road
53. Belief
54. 10th day of Christmas fellas
58. Horse house
62. Mr. Tarkenton
63. Eat away
64. Tied
65. Powdered fruit drink
66. Big book
67. Aida, e.g.

DOWN

1. M.P. command
2. Past due
3. 1996 campaigner
4. Favorite holiday carol
5. *Harold and* ___
6. Sights in
7. Spinning toy
8. Mr. Capote
9. Red nosed reindeer
10. Everyone has one
11. "Like father, like ___ "
12. *Cloak and Dagger* director
14. Indulges
18. Cart
20. "Aida," for one
22. "One if by ___ "
23. Heap
24. Police org.
25. Cook classic
26. Fort Worth campus; abbr.
27. Approves
29. Sot sound
31. "Deck the ___ "
34. Actress Patricia, et al.
35. " ___ the Season . . ."
36. 4-F
37. Sled jinglers
38. Skate move
39. Buzzards Bay campus; abbr.
40. Early photo illuminator
43. Alas in Hamburg
44. Tit for ___
45. The Chaneys
47. Scrooge coin
48. " ___ there, done that"
49. Form a contract
51. Duck walk
53. Christmas tag word

🌴 *Belle's Nöel* 🌴

54. Not right
55. Theme girl from *Doctor Zhivago*
56. Receive
57. Spanish gold
59. Volcano output
60. M. Div., often
61. SSW opposite

Six

BELLE was in the kitchen deeply engrossed in a cookbook when Rosco walked in with Sara Briephs. As neither he nor Belle felt comfortable with the grand old lady driving home alone at night, he'd opted to journey to her house on Newcastle's tony Patriot Hill to pick her up for dinner. These "chauffeured outings"—Sara's term—were the only instances in her long life in which she had absolutely no say. Given her indomitable spirit, it's doubtful she would have permitted anyone other than Belle and Rosco to regulate her activities, but Sara was notoriously soft-hearted where "the youngsters" were concerned. In fact, she believed they could do absolutely no wrong.

"Two teaspoons crumbled thyme. Check," Belle was mumbling to herself while the white-haired dowager airily perched herself atop one of the kitchen stools—another behavioral anomaly. Sara seldom spent time in her own kitchen, let alone ensconced herself among its homey furnishings. And now seated atop this Fifties' retro perch, she resembled a life-sized, vintage doll whose feet didn't quite reach the floor.

"One cup tomato juice. Done. Three sprigs parsley. Got that. One bay leaf . . ." Belle droned on.

"Is that the promised Yankee pot roast you're concocting, dear? The aroma is positively ambrosial."

"Let's hope it's as good as it smells." Belle looked up from her book; more than a little pride showed on her face. Because she was no cook, her forays into chefdom were grand events—although, as everyone knew, the results were often less than perfect. Aside from the infamous tuna casserole, with no tuna, there'd been a certain red-hot meatloaf she'd concocted when she'd first fed her then husband-to-be.

"No hot chili pepper flakes, I hope?" he now asked with a nervous smile and a hint of sarcasm.

She glanced at the cookbook again and frowned as she scanned the list. "The recipe doesn't call for them, but . . ."

"Mmmm . . ." He nodded.

". . . But, if you think I should-" Then she caught his eye, and recognized his lack of sincerity. "That meatloaf recipe listed red pepper among the ingredients, Rosco. How was I to know it meant red *bell* peppers?"

"A natural mistake," Sara offered. "I would have done the same."

Rosco rolled his eyes and chuckled. "If you two were left to your own devices, you'd starve."

"As long as one's larder is stocked with plenty of tinned foodstuffs, one does not starve, young man," said Sara with some asperity. "Sardines, for instance—"

"And anchovies," tossed in Belle.

"And smoked oysters," continued Sara. "And let me see . . . artichoke hearts and button mushrooms and hearts of palm—"

"You sound like you're describing canapés in the hors d'oeuvre selection at the Patriot Yacht Club, rather than the fixings for a solid meal," Rosco observed.

"Nothing wrong with canapés," Sara sniffed. "Many a yacht club member has made a full dinner from the chef's nibbles. Your wife is addicted to deviled eggs, which certainly fall into the canapé category. And look how hale and hearty she is."

There was no gainsaying this argument. Belle, despite being able to consume an entire plateful of deviled eggs at one sitting, was the picture of rosy-cheeked health. Rosco gave his wife an adoring hug as Sara abruptly changed the subject—another advantage of being eighty-plus. "I'm worried about Martha," she stated.

"Martha?" Belle asked as she spooned vegetable-studded brown gravy over the cooking pot roast. "We saw her this afternoon at the dog park. She looked fine. A little worried about Princess, but—"

"It's not Martha's physical well-being that concerns me. Nor her dog's."

Both Belle and Rosco turned toward Sara and waited for her to continue. One didn't rush a person as regal and autocratic as Mrs. Briephs. "You know, of course, that we're fellow participants in the church sewing group?"

Belle nodded. She'd also been asked to join "Sisters in Stitches," but she was no more expert with a needle than she was with a Newburg sauce.

"Well, we 'girls' were all talking about holiday plans during our latest gathering—visiting family and friends, parties, and so forth—when Martha suddenly exclaimed that she had no intention of celebrating Christmas this year. 'All this hoopla. The season's just about overeating and regretting it later,' is how she put it. She even told us she was sorry Lawson's wasn't open on Christmas itself, because she thought the day should be treated as just one out of three hundred sixty-five."

Belle nodded. She could imagine Martha using those very words. She was a person who didn't believe in beating around the bush.

"I told her that she was spouting nonsense, of course, and that the holidays were about sharing and showing our love for one another."

"And?" Belle asked.

"And she said that if we truly cared for one another we wouldn't need a special time of year to prove it. We'd do it every day."

"She's got a point," Rosco agreed.

"Well, of course she has a point, dear boy. A very good one, too. But the problem isn't whether Martha is right or wrong in her assessment, it's her motive that bothers me. Anyone who claims that Christmas should be viewed as merely another day seems determined to be unhappy."

"She was her usual cheery self this afternoon," Belle protested. "I saw nothing 'Scroogey' about her, at all."

"The self each of us shows the world is not necessarily who we truly are," was Sara's quiet response.

Belle and Rosco looked at their aging friend. It seemed inconceivable that she could be anyone other than who she appeared to be: a strong-willed woman whose ancestors had been among the city's forebears and whose wise heart was made of the purest gold.

"You regard me as a bossy old bat, for instance; when I think I'm still an eighteen-year-old hellion who's masquerading as an adult. The face I see in my mirror is a constant surprise—and not always a pleasant one."

"Well, you've fooled us," Rosco chuckled. "I would have said you were definitely an adult."

"I see you make no comment on my 'bossy old bat' status," Sara observed with a smile, then brought the conversation back to Martha. "She needs a gentleman in her life."

"A gentleman—?" Rosco began.

"Too old-fashioned a term, dear boy? I forget that we *antiques* sometimes use obsolete phraseology. Simply put: She needs to start dating again. She's only fifty-two; she can't devote the rest of her life to a *dog*."

At this moment, Kit and Gabby, who'd been peaceably sleeping on the kitchen floor, leapt up and started barking.

"Quiet girls," Belle ordered, then turned back to Sara. "I assume you've got a scheme all figured out whereby Martha gets her guy—"

Kit and Gabby interrupted again, flying out of the kitchen and racing through the living room to Belle's office, where they took up an angry guardianship of the door leading to the garden.

"Indeed I do have a 'scheme,' my dear," Sara answered as though the air were not filled with furious woofs and snarls. "The traditional Secret Santa we always have at the toy-wrapping party. We simply arrange it so that—"

"But the gift exchange is just luck of the draw," Rosco said skeptically. "You can't *rig* it—"

"Oh, no? It's *my* house in which we're having the festivities this year. Therefore *my* rules apply."

"You're not suggesting something illicit?" Rosco jested.

"Legality doesn't enter into it. What I'm proposing is strictly practical. I put every name in the hat except two—"

"And who are you targeting as Martha's Secret Santa and clandestine admirer?" Belle asked with a grin.

"Why, Stanley Hatch, naturally."

Rosco shook his head. "I don't know, Sara. He may not be ready just yet—"

"Nonsense. Besides, I'm only suggesting *friendship* for two lonely people—"

"But they may not want—"

"I've already made up my mind. I'll assign Stanley to Martha and vice versa. Didn't you tell me that their two *dogs* get along?" With a touch of facetiousness, she added, "What more does anyone need?"

"Well . . ." Belle began and looked at Rosco.

"If you think I'm too aged to discuss the vagaries of sex-appeal, young lady, I'm not. But affection and love must have a basis in friendship and respect. Stanley's alone and gloomy; Martha's alone and despondent. If they develop nothing more than a comfortable companionship, that's fine. But I'll bet you dollars to doughnuts that one day we'll see something more. And if you're concerned my little stratagem will be discovered, I assure you it won't—unless one of you gives me away. And I further pledge that those will be the only names I fix—"

The dogs interrupted with renewed vigor, and Rosco was suddenly alert. "What's going on? This isn't like them—" The words died in his throat. "The back door's locked, isn't it?"

He glanced at Belle, who nodded. "And the front door?"

"Well, you and Sara came in that way—"

"Stay here." Rosco hurried into the living room. The two women could hear him rifling through the coat closet. "Lock the door behind me, all right?"

As Belle walked toward the main entry, she saw the revolver in his hand. Despite Rosco's work as a private detective, it was something he carried only on rare occasions. "What's this all about?"

The dogs anxious barking increased, but neither Belle nor Rosco turned toward the sound.

"I'll be right back," he said. "And don't let the girls follow me."

Belle did as she was asked, but she needn't have worried about Kit and Gabby. Neither one relinquished her post beside the office door. In fact, they seemed not to have heard Rosco leave by the front door—which was unusual in the extreme.

"A prowler?" Sara asked, joining Belle, who merely shook her head in confusion.

Minutes passed, punctuated by growls and spates of ferocious barking. Then, finally, Rosco returned by way of the rear door.

"Are you going to tell us what the problem is?" Belle asked.

He hung up his jacket and returned his revolver to its hiding place. He seemed unwilling to speak. "There was a prison break this morning . . . near Boston . . . a long way away, I know . . ." As he searched for words, Kit and Gabby were pawing at his trouser legs, all apparent worry gone. They greeted him as if he'd just returned from a mundane workday and were now preparing to devote himself solely to their canine concerns.

"Well, whatever was bothering those two seems to be forgotten," Belle observed with a small smile.

"Probably a neighbor's cat—or a raccoon nosing around the trash bin," Sara stated. "Besides, no escaped criminal would come south, Rosco. The entire northeast corridor is far too densely populated for a serious vanishing act. If I were on the lam, I'd go to Maine—and thence to Canada—"

"Where you'd hide in a snowbound cabin and subsist on hearts of palm and deviled ham," Rosco couldn't resist tossing in.

"Perhaps a box or two of Melba toast would be a wise addition," Sara replied, before continuing to "hatch" her Yuletide conspiracy. Belle pulled the covered iron casserole dish from the oven, and Rosco proceeded to set the table for dinner while Kit and Gabby curled up on the kitchen floor.

"Oh, I meant to tell you, dear," Sara warbled while her friends made their final dinner preparations. "I glanced at your *"Belle's Nöel"* contest puzzle in the *Crier* before I left home tonight—"

"She can't be bribed, Sara," Rosco joked. "I already tried."

"My dear boy, I'd never consider such unlawful behavior."

Seven

THE sky the next morning was an ominous gray, and a blustery wind from the northwest made the twenty-four degree temperature feel more like ten, but there still was no snow in the forecast. Al, Rosco and Abe had returned to the NPD evidence room at eight A.M. and once again suited up in their Santa costumes. Belle had pinned miniature Christmas trees and plastic holly leaves to a red, fleece dog jacket so that Gabby could also share in the holiday finery, and the three humans and single canine were back at it: collecting the gift toys the Newcastle merchants had gathered.

"Six or seven inches of snow would be nice right about now," Abe remarked as they loaded a cart full of goodies retrieved from Gilbert's Groceries into the back of the unmarked police van. "Well, maybe it would be better if it held off until we get these toys delivered to the kids. But then . . ."

"Forget about it," Al said, tossing a football to Rosco, who stood in the back of the van with Gabby. "This ain't gonna be no white Christmas. Weatherman's predicting clear skies all week; which is fine by me. You two winter-sports bums can keep the snow." He grabbed another football, took four or five steps backward, looked right, then left, and passed it into Rosco. Gabby leapt up in an attempt to intercept it. "You know, if we played for the Pats," Al continued, "we'd be down in Tampa Bay right now getting ready for tomorrow's game. Eighty degrees, sunshine, warm breeze off the Gulf . . ."

"I hate to break it to you, Al, but we don't play for the Pats. And, yes, Abe and I are looking forward to getting in our share of winter sports sometime soon. December's almost over and we haven't had anything resembling a frozen pond or freshly packed ski trail—"

"My heart bleeds." Lever handed the last toy to Rosco. "Speaking of which; your honey sure cooked up a doozy of a crossword competition for the *Crier*. No way am I scoring the 'deluxe dinner for two'—with or without help."

Rosco pointed to the grocery entrance. "How about a 'deluxe' home-cooked job for Helen? You rustle up a nice filet of beef, do the lighted-candle bit, buy her an expensive bottle of champagne—"

"Do I look like a cook to you, Poly—Crates?"

"Well, now that you mention it, Al, you do have a certain chef-like girth . . . Kind of a Paul Prudhomme thing."

"Ho, ho." Al walked off to return the shopping cart to the store while Rosco turned to Abe.

"No snow, huh?"

"Well, I don't know about Christmas, but the *Almanac*'s been predicting a dry and unusually frigid winter when we hit January and February."

"Since when is the *Farmer's Almanac* always right?"

"How about since 1792?"

Rosco considered this sobering piece of information. "Cold, huh?"

"Does the word *arctic* mean anything to you?"

Rosco grimaced and shook his head. "Okie-doke . . . What's our next stop?"

Jones flipped through a few sheets of paper on a stainless steel clipboard and said, "Papyrus, the office supply store on the other side of the interstate. Everything else is to the south, so we might as well start with Papyrus and get it out of the way."

"Sounds reasonable." Rosco picked up Gabby and stepped out of the rear of the van while Abe closed and locked it. Then they circled around to the passenger's side and slid into the front seat; Jones in the middle and Rosco sitting by the door with Gabby on his lap. "Sorry, she goes crazy if she doesn't get the window."

"Buster's the same way. Gotta ride shotgun." Jones slipped on a pair of wrap-around dark glasses, making him look like the heppest Santa north of Rio de Janeiro. "Here's something to consider," he said as he gazed through the windshield. "Do you think dogs understand that we humans are actually *driving* the cars?"

"Huh?"

"I mean, visualize it; we walk toward a car—pooches and people, that is—then we jump into it. As far as dogs are concerned, the backseat is nothing more than another comfy couch, right? While the people settle themselves in the two Bark-O-Loungers up front. The dogs don't bother to wonder what we're doing. Why would they comprehend that we're actually *controlling* the movements of the vehicle?"

Gabby rolled her eyes and let out a low woof, thinking, *Oh, brother. What planet is this guy from?*

Rosco had come to pretty much the same conclusion.

"I mean, even now," Jones continued, "here we are in the van, waiting for Al, and Gabby doesn't know what the heck's going on . . . No offense, Gabsters, but you don't. Then, all of a sudden, Al opens the door and slides in behind the wheel; and the van mysteriously starts making noises. Then it begins to roll forward. How would Gab understand that Al is actually causing the movement?"

"I think you've got more time on your hands than you should, Abe. Either that, or you're sniffing too much formaldehyde down in the forensics lab."

"No, I'm convinced my theory's right, Rosco. That's why Buster gets so anxious and excited when I pick up my car keys; he thinks the darned thing's going to leave without us if we don't hurry up and get out of there."

Gabby hunkered down into Rosco's lap as if she were terrified she was sitting beside a madman.

"You see, Polycrates, your problem is that you accept things as they seem on the surface. You've got to dig deeper. It's like when I go to the video store with Buster and look for a movie. As far as he's concerned, I'm just staring at the wall as if I were some sort of idiot. How could he have any concept of reading? About making a choice? How would he know that I'm trying to decide between a Jennifer Lopez film and a Sandra Bullock film?"

"You're right, I'd find that scenario baffling, myself."

"I can see I'm getting nowhere with you."

"Well, here comes Al. Why don't you run the notion past him. He tends to be more open-minded than I am."

"Right," Jones said sarcastically. "By the way, how's the perfect gift for your own little lovebird coming along? You're all squared away on that?"

"I still have a logistical problem, but I'm working on it."

"And . . . ?"

"It's still a state secret."

Lever slid in behind the wheel and started the van. Rosco and Abe looked down at Gabby for a reaction, but she opted not to give them the satisfaction of a response. Instead, she stared intently ahead.

"Where to?" Al asked.

"Papyrus," Rosco and Abe said in unison.

"Got it."

Lever eased the van into traffic, drove up the street for eight blocks, entered the interstate ramp, and headed north. The conversation between the three men revolved around how well the Pats might fare against the Tampa Bay Buccaneers, while Gabby ignored them and concentrated on the passing scenery. After five or six miles, Al glanced into the rearview mirror and said, "We're being tailed."

"Huh?" Abe said.

"We've got a Mass State Trooper on our tail."

"You're kidding? How fast are you going?" Rosco asked.

"Sixty-five . . . maybe seventy."

"This is a fifty-five zone, Al."

"Everyone's going seventy, Poly—crates. Don't tell me you poke along at fifty-five on this stretch." Lever looked again into the mirror. "Oh boy, here we go . . . he's got his flashers on. Did either one of you bring I.D.?"

"It's all back in my street clothes," Jones said.

Rosco followed with, "Me, too. You mean you didn't bring your driver's license, Al?"

"There's no pockets in these costumes, all right?" He began angling the van over to the breakdown lane. "I don't see either one of you clowns with a wallet, either."

"Huh," Abe said with a laugh. "We can't even bribe this guy."

"Don't worry, I can talk our way out of this," Lever announced with a bit of false bravado. "I know how to handle these guys." He brought the van to stop as the trooper's cruiser pulled up and idled thirty feet behind them. Al opened the door, but before he could step out, the state trooper was on his bullhorn with a commanding order.

"Sir, stay in the van. Do not exit the vehicle."

Lever looked at Abe and Rosco, and shrugged. Then, ignoring the trooper's request, he popped out of the van, his red plush trouser legs flapping in the icy wind.

The cruiser's door flew open. The trooper leapt out and crouched behind the open window, his gun drawn and pointed straight at the lieutenant. "Get back in the van, fat man. You've got five seconds."

Lever instinctively raised his hands, then did as he was told. "Fat man?" he said incredulously as he slid back into the driver's seat. "Fat man? Who's this guy think he is? Where's he get off with this 'fat man' stuff?" Abe and Rosco were now chortling, which prompted Al to add, "Hey, he's twenty-three years old, max, and he has his weapon drawn. This is no laughing matter. We'd better find out what he's up to." He reached down and turned on the police radio. "What's the Statie's frequency?"

Jones raised an eyebrow. "You're asking me? I'm the lab guy, remember. That's your department."

Rosco reached down and moved the receiver's dial to the Massachusetts State Police frequency. "How do you guys get anything done?" he said, still chuckling.

The radio crackled, and the young trooper's voice echoed through the van's speaker system. He was calling for backup. "I have the suspects . . . locked stationary . . . I-195 at the thirty-eight-mile marker. Canine present in vehicle. I.D. positive. Two Caucasians. One heavyset. One African-American.

All dressed as Santa Claus." A burst of static was followed by, "Backup on the way. Sit tight."

Then the radio barked out further orders. "All units, switch to isolation frequency. Delta-Blue."

"So much for our eavesdropping." Al turned off the radio. "Who comes up with these names? Delta-Blue; sounds like a stripper, if you ask me."

"Mr. Heavyset *weighs* in," Abe gibed.

"Ho, ho . . . At least the guy didn't refer to you as a buff African-American."

Within thirty seconds, all traffic on both sides of I-195 had been shunted off the roadway, making the busy interstate resemble a deserted airport runway. After another thirty seconds, four more state police cruisers appeared in the southbound lane and came to a lurching stop beyond the separating guardrail. Two troopers jumped from each of the vehicles and positioned themselves behind the front and rear fenders, guns drawn and ready for action. Three more cruisers had joined the officer behind the van.

"What do we look like, Bonnie and Clyde?" Lever complained. "I'm going to get out and talk to these guys. Whoever they think we are, they're wrong."

"Hold on, Al," Rosco said, reaching across Abe and placing a hand on the lieutenant's red sleeve. "These guys look serious. Drawn weapons isn't about doing seventy in a fifty-five zone. I'd hate to see someone get nervous and make a mistake. Let's wait them out. Sooner or later they'll run our plates through their computer and realize they've got the wrong guys."

Abe Jones shook his head. "The Staties don't have any record on these being NPD plates—just like we don't know the Blue-Delta frequency. You never know when you'll need to keep official business to yourself." He let out a rueful chuckle. "One big, happy Massachusetts family, right?"

Eight

*I*F the day hadn't started well for Abe, Rosco, and Al Lever, things had begun in an equally hairy fashion at Lawson's Coffee Shop. Kenny, Lawson's head chef, who liked to refer to himself as "a fry cook," but whom regular patrons called "King Kenny" because of his commanding height and demeanor, had arrived at five-thirty A.M. on the dot—just as he had for nearly three decades. Martha, also as usual, had reached the establishment at five-forty-five; and the other waitresses and kitchen help had begun filing in shortly thereafter. But all appearances of normalcy had ended there, because not five minutes after Kenny had unlocked the exterior basement door, it became clear to him that someone had broken into the coffee shop's building.

He was in the midst of suiting up in his whites, an immaculately pressed pair of white cotton trousers and matching jacket, and hanging his street clothes in his locker, when he noticed a curious fact: the basement was icy cold. He crossed to the furnace and checked it, but he found the machine running at a comfortable level. He then turned around in his deliberate and methodical manner and started to survey the entire room. In the still-dim light—Kenny didn't believe in wasting electricity—his dark skin resembled polished jet against the starchy sheen of his uniform, and his stance was princely and authoritative.

"Hi-dee-ho, your majesty," Martha called as she breezed in through the basement door. She stopped and shivered slightly, and Kenny greeted her with a sonorous:

"Something's wrong, Marth. Someone's been in here." He and Martha had worked together for so many years they'd developed a number of nicknames for one another. "Marth" or "Madam M." were favorites of Kenny's, but they took on a somber formality when expressed in his rich baritone.

Martha began flipping on light switches. "Place looks the same to me, Dr. K."

"It's cold, Marth."

"So? It's frigid outside. It's a December kinda thing. The *Almanac* says—"

"The basement is never this cold, doll."

George, the dishwasher, appeared at that moment. Like Rosco, he was part of the city's large Greek-American population; unlike Rosco, he spoke heavily accented English. "Window broke," is all he said, pointing up the cellar stairs he'd just walked down.

Kenny, followed by Martha, who perpetually came to work already attired in her "Lawson's pink," went outside to investigate. The dishwasher followed; a newly arrived waitress, Lorraine, joined them.

Sure enough, a crawlspace window had been displaced. The foursome—which had now grown to five—returned to the basement where they found the lost glass panel. The framing hadn't been broken; it had been merely pushed in—not a difficult task since the putty and wood had grown spongy and useless with age. But the single pane of glass had been shattered when it fell onto the cellar floor.

"Someone did this on purpose," Kenny announced. "It didn't happen on its own."

"But nothing looks disturbed," Martha observed.

The crowd—which was now six—moved upstairs into the restaurant proper where they found the chairs piled upside down on the tables as they always were at the end of a work day.

"Someone other than the cleaning crew was here last night," Kenny stated.

"What's this? E.S.P., Dr. K.? Got your crystal ball fired up this early in the morning?"

"I feel what I feel," was the philosophical reply. "Whether the furniture was disturbed or not, someone marched through here last night. I'll give you odds on that."

Martha raised an ironic eyebrow, but she and the other employees fanned out to investigate. The cash register was checked, although no money ever remained from the day before. The safe appeared untouched, but Mr. Lawson would be the one to confirm that. Kenny and Martha then walked into the kitchen and examined the commercial refrigerator and freezer. Nothing appeared disturbed there either.

"We'll have to call the cops," Kenny said. "And the boss. How to ruin your day off in one easy lesson."

"Enough of the NPD will be here for breakfast the moment we unlock the door," Martha wisecracked. "We'll describe the situation while they're wolfing down their hash and eggs. The boys and girls in blue always work better when their bellies are full."

"It's our duty to report any suspicions of wrongdoing," was Kenny's stern response. "Do you want to call nine-one-one, or should I?"

"Nothing's missing, Dr. K. Maybe it was only the wind last night—or the Ghost of Christmas Past."

"The police should decide that."

"Whatever you say, your majesty. Knock yourself out. As for me, I'm going to get that coffee brewing. It's never a pretty sight when these caffeine fiends turn rabid."

"This is not a joking matter, Marth," Kenny said in admonition.

"And facing a roomful of java-deprived cops who've spent all night on their 'dogs' is?"

THE break-in was duly reported, and the two police officers who responded to the call were then treated to Lawson's enormous breakfasts while several groups of regular patrons speculated as to the perpetrator and cause of the crime. As far as anyone could assess, nothing was missing, as Martha had asserted. The assumption was that Kenny's early arrival had forced the culprit to flee before completing whatever felony he or she had intended.

"All I can say," Martha concluded as she poured a third round of coffee for a table of regulars, "is that whoever had the gall to break in wasn't from around here. There's nothing down in the basement but canned beans and coffee."

"I'll bet you can find more to say if you put your mind to it," one of her patrons quipped.

"You want your coffee in your cup or you want it in your lap?" was her swift response, but another of the group interrupted.

"What makes you think it had to be a stranger, Martha? We have our fair share of shifty folks right here in town."

"Anyone who knows Newcastle knows that Kenny's a nut for punctuality. Come this summer, he will have been here for thirty years. Thirty years of arriving at half-past five, rain or snow or sleet or whatever other muck the Bay State throws at us . . . That's why I'm saying the perp wasn't a local. Plus, who'd mess with Dr. K.? The guy's six-foot-four, for Pete's sake. He might look and act like an emperor in disguise, but he's one tough hombre."

WHEN the breakfast rush had died down and the official police visit had ended, Kenny left his post in the kitchen and ensconced himself at one of the banquette tables where Martha served him coffee and juice accompanied by a running account of that morning's news and gossip. This was their longstanding tradition, but this time Kenny didn't return her bantering tone. "Why are you always joking around?" he asked instead. "You can't laugh off every incident, you know. This could be a very severe situation."

"Hey, you want hangdog, I can do that. Should I march about with a sign reading 'The End Is Near?' "

"I'm serious, Marth."

"So am I. Life's too short to go around acting glum and gloomy."

"I'm not talking about behaving in a dejected manner, I'm talking about sincerity."

Martha put down the coffee carafe. Her customary flippant retort died on her lips; even her blonde, beehive hairdo seemed to crumple while something that could only be described as two tears filled her eyes.

"Because you *are* a sincere person, Marth," Kenny continued in a softer tone. "And a caring one."

Martha screwed up her eyes, shook her head, sniffed, and gave a dismissive shrug. "Caring, shmaring—"

"If you don't open your heart, how can you let people grow close to you?"

"Who says I want anyone to?"

"Everyone needs lovin', Marth," he added.

"Which is why I got Princess," Martha rejoined.

"Human beings require more than just a dog's affection."

"Says you."

"Says my wife." Kenny smiled but didn't speak for a moment. Finally, he said, "I worry about you, Madam M . . . All your friends do; that's all I'm saying."

"Well, you needn't bother. And you don't want to go spouting that nonsense around Princess, either. Talk about hurting someone's feelings. Good thing she didn't hear you."

Nine

"THE Staties must think we're those three idiots who broke out of the Suffolk County Jail." Al Lever slowly rolled his head from side to side as he spoke. "That's the only explanation."

All vehicles were still being diverted from route I-195 at the exits closest to the unmarked police van driven by the three hapless Santas. The seven Massachusetts State Police cruisers—along with the troopers who were maintaining a weapons-drawn stance—continued to hold their position. Traffic was now backed up for six miles in both north- and south-bound lanes, putting those drivers en route to some festive holiday shopping in less than joyous moods.

"One of those jokers was African-American?" Abe asked, removing his dark glasses. The gesture hinted at the fact that he thought this might reveal his true identity despite the snow-white beard, mustache, and wig he continued to wear.

"Yep."

"This is what I get for hanging out with white guys. If I miss the Pats game because I'm sitting in the state police barracks lockup, I'm never speaking to either of you again."

"Hey, come on, Abe," Rosco said with a laugh, "remember, it's all for a good cause."

"And rooting for the Pats isn't?"

"Not if you're from Tampa," was Rosco's response.

"Ho, ho," Lever tossed in, but his tone was mirthless.

"And another one was fat?" Abe continued. "This is too much."

"Just knock it off with the 'fat' stuff, okay?" Al grumbled.

"Sorry, Al, I meant to say heavyset."

"Are the escapees known to be violent?" Rosco shifted Gabby in his lap as he turned to face Al. "What were they in for?"

"I'm trying to remember . . . I think they were awaiting trial."

"Which means they couldn't make bail." Abe observed in a serious tone. "Which means they were dead broke, or more than likely, bail was set too high. Which means they were a flight risk."

"Not necessarily," Rosco objected. A small smile began to play on his lips. "It's possible that they're so horribly violent, such despicable cutthroats, buccaneers, if you will, and are suspected of such heinously sadistic crimes that the state—"

"Thank you, Mr. Helpful," Lever interrupted. "The point is, the Staties have the wrong people. How do we communicate that to them? Now that they've so brilliantly switched off our frequency."

"Okay," Rosco said, "It's simple: We just take off our wigs and beards and exit the vehicle with our hands up. What's the problem? I mean, maybe the fat guy they're looking for isn't bald. Then we're in the clear."

Despite Lever's objection to yet another 'fat' comment, the three men decided to follow this plan of action, pulling off their wigs and detaching the adhesive that held their beards in place. "Okay, Al," Rosco said after they'd removed as much of their holiday disguises as they could. "You'd better step out first."

"Are you nuts? Look at those guys; they're just waiting to make a kill. Two of them are drooling! What's wrong with you, Poly—crates? You go first."

"I've got a dog on my lap. I can't raise my hands. Besides, they can see you better. And to be honest, you look less shifty than Abe and me."

"That is so lame. In fact, it's the lamest excuse I've ever heard—even from you. Hiding behind a dog, and a small one at that . . . Sheesh."

"Rosco's right, Al," Jones protested. "We need to make sure the Staties understand our intentions." He jabbed his elbow into the lieutenant. "Off you go. Be sure to write."

"Ho, ho."

In the end, Lever realized it was the only solution to the standoff. He cautiously opened the door, stepped from the van, hands held high in the air, and shouted, "We're police officers. This is a Newcastle Police Department vehicle."

"Up against the van, fat man," echoed from a bullhorn across the roadway.

Lever looked at Jones, who had replaced him in the driver's seat. "This reference to my size is getting very old," Al mumbled.

The bullhorn continued, "Palms up against the side of the van, wide apart; spread your feet and make no quick moves . . .

Okay, number two, out of the van. Keep those hands where we can see them."

Jones glanced at Rosco. "Number two? Personally, I don't care for the metaphor."

Rosco shrugged. "Hey, what'd you expect? Imagination?"

Abe stepped out of the van and positioned himself next to Al: hands spread, feet wide apart, as Rosco slid across the seat. He placed Gabby next to him and said, "Stay here, Gabs, I'll be right back."

But as Rosco left the van, Gabby also hopped out, then ran to a grassy patch to relieve herself. Rosco made a move to retrieve her, but the bullhorn blared with another warning.

"Don't move. Stay where you are. Do not follow the dog. Up against the van."

Rosco did as he was told, and after a minute Gabby trotted over and sat between his legs.

"Ya gotta go, ya gotta go," Abe said, and Gabby responded with three shorts yips.

The Massachusetts State Police officers descended upon them like a swarm of wasps and had the threesome patted down, handcuffed, and with their backs against the van before anyone could say a word. Gabby growled and yapped during the entire operation until an unusually tall trooper wearing captain's bars on his jacket turned to a shorter officer and barked out an order. "Call Animal Control. Who knows where they stole this mutt from."

Mutt? Gabby thought. *Where's this guy get off? A couple of canine teeth to the back of the leg would teach him a good lesson.* But she opted to let the critique pass; the humans were in enough trouble without complicating the situation.

Lever scanned the dozen or so officers looking for a familiar face, but their crisp uniforms, chiseled faces and muscle-men physiques made them appear disconcertingly similar. It was as if they'd just lockedstepped their way out of one of the boxes of Combat Action Soldiers lying in the back of the van. So Al started from square one.

"Fellas, you've got the wrong men. My name is Lieutenant Al Lever. I'm a homicide detective with the Newcastle Police Department." He cocked his head to his right. "This is Abe Jones, our forensics man, and Rosco Polycrates, a private detective, formerly NPD. It's his dog, and he's got the appropriate medical records and license to prove it. This is a police van. Phone the plates into NPD. Ask for Dolores; she'll confirm everything I'm telling you."

The officers had holstered their weapons by then, and the tall trooper with the captain's bars stood at their center, his hands resting aggressively on his hips. He was the one who spoke, and his tone was flat and unforgiving. "We checked the plates, bozo. They don't come up NPD. Do you have I.D. to substantiate this claim, or are you just wasting taxpayer dollars?"

"I had a feeling you might ask that." Lever sighed. "We're collecting Christmas gifts for kids. We left our I.D. in our street clothes."

"Captain, take a look in the van," Rosco chimed in. "There's a police radio, shotgun bracket; the rear's sealed off for detainees—"

The trooper held up his hand. "I'm not concerned about the van at the moment; right now I want to know who you three yokels are."

"Well, we sure as heck didn't just break out of the Suffolk County Jail," Jones replied, annoyed at being handcuffed for the first time in his life.

"I know that," the trooper stated. "But I didn't until you pulled off the wigs. The skinny guy from Suffolk's bald, and the fat guy's a tattooed biker with a pony tail."

Both Rosco and Al decided it wasn't a good time to protest the "skinny" and "fat" descriptions.

"Unless you fellas can prove who you are," the captain continued, "I'm going to have to take you back to the barracks. Animal Control will be here in a minute for the dog."

At this suggestion, Gabby once again began barking and growling at the trooper. "Aw, come on, captain," Rosco protested over the noise, "this makes no sense. You're serving yourself up a mountain of paperwork, and we won't get these gifts to the kids on time. Why don't you just get an NPD beat-cop to drive out here and 'make' us. It'll take ten minutes."

Rosco's idea made a certain amount of sense to the captain, but he wasn't about to make life that easy for the Santas.

"I've got three potentially violent criminals on the loose. There's no telling where they are. They've stolen a car; they've cleaned out a costume shop, so I don't know what the hell they're dressed up as; and you think I'm worried about paperwork?"

"What makes you think they moved this far south, Captain?" Lever asked, now sounding businesslike, and very much the detective.

"One of them apparently has a sister in Newcastle." The captain then looked at the trooper standing beside him. "Roberts, contact NPD. See if they can send someone out here to vouch for these clowns." He glanced at Al. "Where did you leave your I.D.?"

Lever sighed again. "In the evidence room."

The captain nodded; it was clear he considered Al's response less than professional. Then he addressed a second trooper. "Shaw, cite the bald one for driving without a license, and the skinny one with a leash violation."

"Come on, Captain," Lever groaned, "that's petty garbage and you know it."

The captain smiled at Shaw. "Write the big guy up for doing seventy in a fifty-five while you're at it."

Ten

WHEN the three Santas entered Don Oliver's Gun Shoppe at eleven-thirty on Thursday morning, Don, the thirty-two-year-old owner was waiting for them. The Santas appeared a good deal less cheery than they had an hour earlier. Their costumes were rumpled, and their wigs and beards appeared bedraggled and askew. Gabby was nowhere to be seen.

"Hey. I was expecting you guys to stop by yesterday," Don said with a smile. Because he was finishing up with a customer, he only gave the men in red a cursory glance. "Much better getups this year. I'm glad you opted to return to Mr. Claus. Those mice outfits from a year back were for the birds. Whose idea were they anyway?" It was a rhetorical question. Don expected no answer, and he received none. "Let me get Charlie here on his way, and I'll be right with you."

It took Oliver another three or four minutes to ring up the sale, complete the necessary paperwork, and package the new bolt-action 30.06 hunting rifle for his customer. Charlie exited the store, and Don turned his back on his visitors and filed the credit card slip in his cash drawer. He then pointed to a small stack of toys that sat on the rear shelf next to a display of shotgun shells.

"Sorry, guys, but it's not a very good haul this year. I tried to get the customers to stay away from toy guns, like you suggested, but I think a few people took offense. We don't get the teddy-bear crowd in here. It's too bad; I probably could have sold a dozen BB guns if you had a different viewpoint on weapons and who should own them."

"We ain't into no viewpoints, pal," the skinny Santa growled. His name wasn't Rosco; it was Cooper, and he'd been awaiting trial on assault charges in the Suffolk County Jail before he and his two compatriots made their break.

Before Oliver had time to respond or even move, Cooper lunged across the glass countertop, cupped his hand over Don's mouth, vaulted a freestanding handgun-and-hunting-knife display case, and wrestled the shop owner to the floor. Don made an attempt to press his silent police alarm, but Cooper twisted his arm behind his back, making the effort impossible.

The black Santa, who went by the name of Lee and was in for armed robbery, trotted to the front door and locked it, while the fat Santa—Scraggs—who'd been awaiting trial on a murder charge, produced a roll of duct tape and dropped it over the counter to Cooper who was still on the floor restraining Don Oliver. The entire operation took the men fifty seconds.

"Tape his mouth, hands, and feet, and make sure he doesn't get near that alarm button again," Scraggs ordered. He peered down at Don. "Don't worry fella; we ain't gonna hurt you . . . as long as you don't make no trouble. All we need is a little hardware, and we'll be outta your hair before you know it."

"He's got himself a second panic button," Cooper said. "It's right here under the cash register." He tugged at Don's twisted arm. "That ain't nice, mister."

"Drag him down to the far end of the counter, so's he can't get at either one of them. And tape his feet to that table so's he can't crawl back down here no time soon."

Cooper did as he was told as Scraggs began studying the weapons in a wall-mounted display case.

"I don't see nothin' here I like," he groused. "I don't want no rifle."

Lee hopped behind the counter and tried to open the case. "It's locked."

"Well, smash the friggin' glass, then," Cooper said. "Let's just grab something and get outta here."

"Ten'll get you twenty if this case is alarmed, you idiot," Lee grumbled. He made no attempt to conceal the fact that he'd be happier without the other two cons. "Ask the punk where he keeps the keys." He raised his voice to be certain Don could hear him. "If he don't tell ya, bash his head in."

Lee's menacing tone was enough to convince Oliver that there was no sense in putting up a fight. Through a series of head and shoulder movements, he indicated that the keys were in his left, front trouser pocket at the end of a chain hanging from his belt. Cooper yanked on the chain, ripping off the belt loop in the process, then returned to the case and unlocked it. "I say we each grab .32s. That way were usin' the same ammo . . . like in case one of us don't make it."

"Hell, you ain't as dumb as you look," Scraggs said with a chuckle, but the sound was sadistic.

Lee made no response to Cooper's suggestion; instead, he pulled a Glock 9mm from the case, retrieved a box of shells from the lower shelf, and began loading it. "You two yokels grab what you want. Me, I'm takin' somethin' I'm comfortable with. 'Cause as soon as I can find me a decent set of wheels, I'm changin' outfits and splittin' from you two. Jolly old Saint Nick and the Salvation Army line can only get you so far in this world. Besides, the cops are probably onto us by now."

"I'm tellin' ya, Lee," Cooper insisted as he grabbed a revolver out of the case, "my sister lives nearby. She'll put us up for a bit. And we don't need to be scroungin' for no food no more neither. She's a good cook, too."

"I take back my earlier comment, Cooper," Scraggs remarked. "You're dumber than dirt. Your sister's joint's gonna be the first place the cops start lookin'."

"Naw, she's got a different last name. Trust me, the cops don't know nothin' about her."

"Hand me that .357 and some ammo, and let's get the hell outta here," was Scraggs' blunt reply. "Lee's right, we need to locate us some new wheels and kill the jolly old elf."

THE "real" Santas, with Gabby at their side, missed the escapees by less than five minutes. When they entered Don Oliver's Gun Shoppe everything seemed perfectly normal—except that Don was nowhere in sight.

"That's odd," Al said as he looked around the store, "Guess he must be in the john." He strolled to the fishing section and removed a large saltwater lure from a wall display. "Don't ever buy one of these babies. I tried one last summer and didn't catch jack."

"You're kidding me," Abe said, attempting to keep a straight face beneath his newly replaced beard. "I've got that exact same lure. I couldn't keep the stripers off it. And sea bass? I had to give them away."

"Ho, ho. You don't even fish, you jerk."

Rosco laughed. "Neither of us do, Al. I wouldn't know a fishing lure from a Kewpie doll. In fact, all those feathers make them look kind of like—"

He was interrupted by a curious thumping noise coming from behind the far end of the sales counter. The three men moved toward the sound, where they found Don, his mouth gagged, his hands bound, and his feet taped securely to a heavy, metal work desk. Gabby, mistaking this for some type of human game of hide and seek, began licking his face, which prompted Rosco to pick her up.

"Not now, girl."

Jones bent down and began removing duct tape from Don's arms and legs, while Lever phoned NPD headquarters. Once the shop owner was on his feet, but before removing the tape from his mouth, Abe asked, "How long have you been like this?"

Don held up both hands and spread his fingers.

"Ten minutes?"

Don double-checked his watch and nodded.

"Okay," Abe said, "I just wanted to be certain the tape hadn't been there for a few hours. Depending on the brand, removal can be a nasty experience. But I think we're okay, as long as we take it nice and easy."

Jones slowly pulled the tape from Don's mouth, holding only the corners. After he'd finished, he attached the tape to a large, plasticized card that identified "The Ducks of North America" in full-color detail. "We should be able to lift some fingerprints off this—if the perp wasn't wearing gloves."

"It wasn't one guy. It was three," Don said, stretching his lips as if he were trying to remember how it felt to talk. "I thought it was you when they walked in, and I—"

"There were three of them?" Lever repeated half to Don and half into the receiver.

"Yeah. Three Santas . . . I don't usually let my guard down like that, but from across the room they looked just like you guys. One of them was even faaa . . . heavyset."

Al gritted his teeth slightly and returned his full attention to the telephone. "Yeah . . . it looks like the clowns who skipped from Suffolk County . . . meaning they're in our jurisdiction, still together, still dressed as Santa Claus—and now armed and dangerous. Let's seal off the area as best we can. According to Oliver, they should only have a five-minute jump on us." He cupped the receiver. "Did you get a make on their vehicle, Don?"

"It was a green sedan; I didn't get the make. It looked like your wife's car, Rosco, that's why I didn't pay much attention . . . I'm usually pretty good about noting who drives what into my lot. You can't be too careful in this business. We can check the security camera. That should give us some answers. Maybe a plate number if we're lucky."

"Do that, will you?" Lever said. "I'd like to see if it matches what the Staties have been looking for."

In the end, all the pieces fit—which meant that it made little sense for Abe, Rosco, and Al to parade around Newcastle dressed in the same outfits as dangerous criminals. So Lever phoned NPD once more and asked to have their street clothes and I.D.s brought out to the gun shop.

"Well, there are only four more merchants on our list," Rosco said, "but it kind of takes the fun out things, going around in civvies. I think the store owners get a kick out of watching us make fools of ourselves."

Lever shrugged and pointed to the telephone. "Hey, it's not too late to get a squad car to hustle up the Three Blind Mice."

Eleven

"Y OU'VE got to be kidding! They were actually mistaken for three cons on the lam?" Martha clasped the collar of her coat tighter to her neck and looked across the bare grounds of the deserted Dew Drop Inn to where Princess, Winston, and Kit were cavorting during a mid-afternoon outing. Despite the fact that Lawson's was open for lunch, its head waitress had chosen to play hooky for the afternoon. She tried to tell herself she was in the park with Belle and Bartholomew Kerr because it was what Princess wanted. But the truth was that Kenny's words of counsel still stung; and Lawson's peculiar break-in still remained unnerving. And both situations merely furthered her belief that Christmas wasn't all it was cracked up to be.

"I would have given a million bucks to see the look on Big Al's face when that went down. It must have been as red as his outfit. What did the Staties think our boys were doing with the toys they were collecting? Planning to fence them at Kiddie Kingdom?" She gave a "Martha" cackle, but the sound was oddly hesitant and uncertain.

Belle shook her head, her face still lined with concern. "Rosco only said they'd been given a rough time of it when he phoned to tell me he'd be late returning."

Bartholomew Kerr tilted his bespectacled head in the manner of a man for whom life has turned unexpectedly grave. "And then stumbling upon the tail-end of the gun shop heist? Committed by the self-same bogus Messers Claus? Thank Heaven there were no injuries. This is not the work of the winged seraphim and cherubim we normally associate with the season—"

"Maybe the holiday spirit's about grabbing rather than giving," Martha rejoined with another short, brash laugh. "But I have to admit, the thought of six grown men dressed up as Santa Claus and having a knock-down drag-out brawl might be a huge draw in the pro wrestling circuit—the Slammin' Santas take on the Kris Kringle Krushers." Then she clamped her mouth shut in a motion that was decidedly atypical. "I'm sorry, Belle honey, I didn't mean to be snide. You're worried about your hubby, and you should be. Goons like those on the loose—and armed—in Newcastle. We should all be a little more worried."

"You weren't being snide, Martha," was Belle's perplexed and gentle answer. "You were simply being yourself."

"Yeah, well . . . sometimes 'being yourself' ain't so hot."

" 'To thine own self be true,' " Bartholomew intoned in his delicate voice, " 'And it must follow as the night the day, Thou cans't not then be false to any man.' *Hamlet*, Act I, Scene III."

"Yeah . . . well . . ." Martha repeated as she shrugged. " 'To be, or not to be'—me. That's what I'm wrestling with." She drew her coat closer to her body. "Sure is cold today."

"Too cold to snow," Bartholomew added. "Which is a shame. I do so love a white Christmas. So does Winston. His Flex-flyer sled comes out of storage, and he rides like the prime minister as we carol the eve away."

Martha's mouth turned downward at this cheery pronouncement. Noticing the expression, Belle remembered what Sara had shared with her, and how worried the old lady was about this seemingly tough-skinned woman. "Did you both receive Sara's e-mailed instructions about the Secret Santas for the gift-wrapping party?" Belle asked to brighten the mood.

"Every *bell* and whistle she attached to her missive," Bartholomew stated. "Pardon the pun, my dear *Anna-gram*, but I couldn't resist. Some octogenarians would throw up their hands at having to become computer literate, but not our Sara. She seems bent on outdoing Mr. Gates himself."

Martha's response was another lackluster shrug. "Yeah, I got the e-mail, but I'm not certain I'm going to be able to attend the party."

"Not go to Sara's?" Belle was incredulous. "But you never work evenings, do you?"

Martha shook her head "no." "I may I have other plans—"

"What other plans?" Belle blurted out.

"My niece—"

"I thought your niece and her husband were visiting his folks in Florida this year."

"Well, there may be a change in their arrangements," Martha lied; and both Belle and Bartholomew could see straight through this bit of deceit.

"It's not going to tarnish your trenchant, Garbo-esque image to celebrate the holidays, Martha," Bartholomew enjoined with some warmth. She turned to him, a look of wounded surprise on her face.

"Is that how you see me? As . . . as 'trenchant'?"

Unaware of how much damage his remark had caused, Bartholomew chortled blithely. "You're right to take me to task. Garbo was not an apt analogy. You're far more of a wisenheimer—let us say, a Bette Midler type. And since my business is chronicling the escapades of people who work overtime to construct newsworthy personae, I'd say you've crafted a very neat public image . . . and one that we all love, I might add, just like the Divine Miss M."

But this single word "love" produced even more anguish. Martha turned away in order to prevent the others from seeing the tears that were filling her eyes. "Look at Princess," she said with false cheer, "and Winston and Kit—all playing together completely unaware that there are problems in the world. A 'dog's life,' that's what they say, isn't it?" Then she blew her nose and repeated her remark about how very cold it was. "When I come back, in my next life, I want to be your pooch, Bartholomew."

"Don't tell me you want to 'go to the dogs,' my dear Miss M.," was Bartholomew's amused reply, then he turned to Belle. "Speaking of dogs and dogged determination, I hear your *Crier* competition's causing a good deal of anguish among puzzle aficionados this year. Or perhaps, given recent events I should say, it's producing a considerable *stir*."

"Pro or *con?*" Martha couldn't help but quip, and Bartholomew beamed up at her.

"Good for you, Miss M. You see how much more fun it is to have the gift of human thought. Now, I don't wish to *hound* you, but our four-legged friends are simply not capable of producing anything resembling your ready wit."

* * *

AT this point, the canines in question were not concerned with humor or wit—or even fun. Instead, they were in the midst of a troubling powwow. Winston, during one of his "peregrinations" with "Old Bug-eye"—the journeys being accomplished by auto rather than by foot—had noticed that the pair of lovebirds in the pet shop window were no longer on display. "And you know what that means, don't you?" he concluded with his chesty growl.

"Rosco can't have purchased them . . ." Kit also growled, but the sound was defensive. In fact, it was almost a whine.

"I'm afraid there can be no other conclusion—"

"But bringing birds into our home, Winston! What could he be thinking of? He knows Gabby and I have no use for them!"

"Does he?" This was Princess' question, and it was voiced in one quick, breathless yip while her petite body in its gumdrop-hued coat skipped in the air.

"Of course, he does . . . Well, I think he does . . . He should . . . What I mean to say is that all humans must have recognized that they can't mix predatory types, i.e., canines, with their natural prey. Surely, Rosco has noticed Gabby and I chasing after the pigeons, crows, and geese that descend into the landscape of this park? Birds have the sky; they have tree limbs; they have rooftops. And that's where they belong."

"Ahhh . . ." Winston's rotund body rocked from side to side. He looked as though he were shaking himself dry, but the action helped stimulate his brain cells. "And do you truly believe the two-legged creatures are that intelligent, Kitty? I've heard stories of them bringing turtles and even fish into their homes. Fish? Can you imagine?"

"Well, humans can drive cars, can't they?"

"Are you suggesting that's that a sign of wisdom—given their obvious need for exercise?"

"I'm not touching that line," Princess yipped, as she eyed Winston's sizable girth.

He ignored the comment while Kit produced another weak growl. "Well . . . they know how to open tin cans and refrigerator doors. They can't be as foolhardy as you're suggesting."

"I believe you've proved the point I'm attempting to make, Madame Kit: Humans invent nasty things like diets precisely because they have easy access to an overabundance of foodstuffs." He looked at Princess. "Lawson's eatery, where your Martha toils, is a case in point, wouldn't you say, my dear? I've heard tales of waffles, French toast, pancakes, fried potatoes . . . the list goes on." Winston heaved a sigh, although whether from envy or censure was uncertain.

Princess squealed her agreement with Winston's assessment while Kit did a brief, uncertain dance step and began scrabbling at the frozen dirt with two unhappy paws. "But what are we going to *do?*" she all but yowled.

"Ahh, there's the rub," Winston woofed. "Well, I suggest you show them the disdain you feel for all forms of avian life." The tone was assured and masterful. He shook himself once more.

"But *how,* if we don't have any birds in the house? If Rosco hasn't even made the connection between Canadian geese and lovebirds . . ." Kit whimpered, "which does seem dense . . . I suppose I could try to catch one of the feathered beasts in the garden. Belle keeps a feeder out there all winter—"

But Winston, as usual, had a better plan. "You mean to tell me that Belle and Rosco don't keep eiderdown-filled pillows upon their bed? Bartholomew does. And he has many more arrayed in the sitting room. He also has a quilt, which he and I enjoy during the cooler months. My point is, my dear Kit, these items are filled with feathers. And where do feathers come from, I might ask?"

Kit cocked her head to one side. Winston's suggestion seemed bold indeed. "You want me to—?"

But Princess interrupted. "Chew them up, dearie. A few feathers on the tongue may taste ticklish and dry at first, but your humans are bound to catch on."

"And if they don't," Winston concluded, "then I fear for the future of their race. A clearer message, one could never hope for." But further appendices to this hypothesis were curtailed by a sudden and quite vicious snarl that seemed to emanate from beneath the broken floorboards of the Dew Drop Inn's ruined porch. "What on earth is that?" the bulldog demanded.

The sound repeated itself as Winston, Kit, and Princess walked toward the stairs leading up to the ancient porch.

"There's a dog hiding under there!" Princess, being the smallest of the three, peered into a crack in stair's lowest riser. "A dirty one, too. Yellow and very big. Bigger than Kit, anyway."

"Get off my turf!" a sinister growl ordered.

"This property belongs to all of us, my dear sir," Winston retorted, "or is it madam?"

"Do I sound like a female, you prig?" The growl grew in intensity. "Don't make me come out there and show you what's what. I'm telling you to hit the road, and I mean it. I've had enough of listening to the whimpers and whines of the pampered elite for one day."

"But—" Winston began."

"Scram!"

The snarl was so loud that Kit was certain the humans

could hear, but when she looked in their direction they seemed oblivious.

"Get lost, you dimwits! And don't come near this burrow again. Ever. This is my spread."

"Strays," Princess sniffed as the four-legged threesome marched back to their two-legged companions. "They can be such unpleasant creatures. I suppose more should be done to find them decent homes, but who wants to share a dwelling with something like *that?*"

"It's awfully cold without a toasty house to return to," Kit mused with a purring sigh.

And although Belle hadn't a clue as to the opinion being given, she inadvertently echoed it. "Our three buddies must be as chilled as we are. They look as though they're asking to be taken home."

Her remark caused Winston to raise his heavy head. "Hardly *puzzling* given the temperature," he snorted to Princess, who returned the gibe with a yipping:

"Don't be cross, Winnie. It's us canines who usually have the final *word.*"

ACROSS

1. Mild oath, dog-wise
4. Dog ___ ; baboon
7. Nose out?
12. ___ Dawn Chong
13. Chew up
15. Illinois river town
16. Rin Tin Tin's network
17. German admiral
18. Brought up
19. Favorite oilman?
22. Verdi opera
23. Oxen collar
24. River in Spain
28. Inventor Nikola
30. Buster's housemate
33. Stanley's housemate
34. Point
35. Black
36. "Cool!"
37. Favorite horse race?
41. 41-Down source
42. Some dog-walkers
43. Royal letters
44. Director Lee
45. Salty dog's domain
46. Old anesthetic
49. Chow
51. Abrade
54. Lemon drinks
56. Favorite Peck film?
60. Dog photo maker
63. ___ blue
64. Ghostly sound
65. "With bated ___ . . .", Shak.
66. Posted
67. ___ dog
68. Jockey wear
69. HST-JFK link
70. A talking horse, et al.

DOWN

1. Persona non ___
2. Dog track tease
3. Encrypt again
4. Mild oath, for Winston
5. Young love in Rome?
6. "with a woof-woof here" refrain
7. Boxer O'Grady
8. Yip, yip, yip, yip
9. Taxing grp.
10. Mild oath
11. Craze
14. Collar locale
15. Tense lead-in
20. Of the snout
21. Actor Edmund, et al.
25. Result of 50-Down
26. Some TVs
27. Wordsmith's vol.
29. Favors one leg
31. Where, and how, to buy meat?
32. Push forth
35. Tiebreakers; abbr.
37. ". . . her poor dog a ___ "
38. With 41-Down, a breakfast order
39. Noah's early dilemma?
40. "Gotcha!", var.
41. See 38-Down
47. Like canned dog food
48. Refill the gun
50. Noise order
52. Dog ___ ; circus highlights
53. Chew up
55. Messes
57. Leftovers

🌴 *If Dogs Made Crosswords* 🌴

58. Cheer

59. Fountain or Rose

60. Lassie's network

61. Uris hero

62. —— Blanc, Wile E. Coyote's voice

ELLE gave Rosco a huge hug the moment he walked through the door. Happy to be home at last, Gabby jumped up and placed her paws on Belle's thighs, received a rather distracted pat, then trotted off into the kitchen for a long drink of water.

"I was so worried about you!" Belle gushed. "What if you three had walked into Don Oliver's a few minutes earlier? You could have found yourselves on the wrong side of those guns."

Rosco gave her a long kiss. "Hey, that's what we were trained for, Belle—stopping felons in the act."

"Not dressed up as Santa Claus, you weren't. I can't believe Al left without his pistol. What was he thinking of?"

"Kids?" Rosco chuckled, but the sound contained as much relief as it did humor. "You're right. The Police Academy rules should specifically outline toy collecting procedure: Don't conduct clandestine operations without a significant means of defending yourself; i.e., make sure your Santa suits have pockets for concealed weapons . . . not to mention I.D. And a clip for handcuffs might be wise, too."

"I'm not joking, Rosco."

"I know. And I'm glad you're not. I much prefer the greet-ing I got, than, say 'What're you doing home so soon, pal?' " He kissed her again. "I do love you, Belle."

"I love you, too . . . but I still wish you'd be more careful."

"Gathering holiday gifts for needy kids isn't supposed to be a high-risk occupation."

"Maybe you should be carrying your gun, too. At least un-til those cons are back in custody." Belle sighed and held him closer. "Everyone was so worried when they heard the news: Bartholomew, Martha—"

"How is everyone's favorite comeback artist, anyway? I'll bet she had some choice observations concerning the Lawson's break-in. 'No warm honey-blueberry syrup today, folks; we've been hit!' "

"No. Oddly she didn't have many wisecracks . . ." Belle paused in thought. "I think Sara's right about Martha . . . something seems to be bothering her—"

"Being subjected to a felony can have nasty side effects, Belle. You don't have to be physically present at the time of the crime to feel violated. And Lawson's is like a second home to Martha—"

"I don't think that's it. Besides, apparently nothing was taken. The police who responded to the call felt that Kenny's arrival put the kibosh on—"

"If it was the same clowns who robbed Don Oliver's Gun Shoppe, our Dr. K. wouldn't have scared them off: six-foot-four or not. Don said these guys were a pretty rough lot."

"Maybe they just wanted some food, and—" Belle stopped, glanced at her watch, and spun around. "Oh, my dog biscuits! I almost forgot . . . the timer should have gone off by now." She flew into the kitchen while Rosco followed at a more reasonable pace.

"You're *baking* dog biscuits? What's wrong with the kind that comes in a red and yellow box? We don't hear many complaints about them from the girls."

Belle didn't respond to his questions. Instead, she whipped a cookie sheet out of the oven. Creative pride sparkled in her eyes. "This batch is banana and peanut butter. Then I'm doing honey and banana. Winston loves bananas— at least according to Bartholomew."

"You're making biscuits from *scratch* for Winston?"

Belle looked at her husband as if he'd lost either his hearing or the momentary use of his brain. "For my Secret Santa gift. Sara's instructions 'suggested' that we 'either find a reasonably priced remembrance or create something handmade.' " Belle slid the finished product onto a cooling rack, then rolled another ball of dough and began stamping out more cookies with a bone-shaped metal cutter.

"And Sara assigned you a *dog?* What's Winston supposed to give the person on his list? Or is a hand-me-down chew toy okay? Maybe something with a little slobber still attached? Or perhaps a molested slipper?"

"Rosco! These are for Bartholomew!"

"I know the man's last name is pronounced 'cur,' Belle, but I didn't think he ate dog food."

"You know, sometimes you are so dense." She chortled, then returned the cookie sheet to the oven and looked at her watch once more. "Twelve minutes . . . I don't know what's wrong with that timer."

Rosco shook the small clock near his ear and said, "You need to wind it up. It works much better that way." He then set it back on the counter, peered into the glass bowl with the remaining dough, and frowned. "I didn't know you could bake cookies. In fact, I didn't think you could bake any-thing."

"I can't," was Belle's breezy reply. "At least I couldn't until just now. I found the cutter in that fancy, new cooking store in town this morning. The owner also supplied two recipes— and *voilà*, or should I say: 'Here you go, matey'—biscuits for the English bulldog, Winston!"

"And how are we going to know if they taste okay?" The question was asked with a certain amount of delicacy. He reached into Kit and Gabby's ceramic jar and removed one of their treats. "Have you ever noticed that these store-bought dog biscuits have the word *Tasty* embossed right on them? See, dogs read that, and they know what they're getting into."

"What, you don't trust me to make dog treats?"

"Well . . ."

"That's it for you, buddy," Belle chuckled. "I was going to add to my repertoire and begin making you gingerbread bones, but you can just forget about it after that crass com-ment."

"Bones? What happened to the traditional 'men'?"

Belle held up the cutter. "I only bought one cookie shape. I considered getting one shaped like a Christmas tree, but then I thought, what would a dog do with a tree?"

"I can only imagine." Rosco then nodded thoughtfully. "And how, may I ask, were you intending on separating Win-ston's, or rather Bartholomew's, gift bones from my bones— the ones I might find edible?"

"I hadn't gotten that far yet," Belle admitted.

This time it was Rosco who chortled. "That's one of my fa-vorite things about you . . . dining is always an adventure." He gave her another tender kiss, but the loving moment was interrupted by the arrival of Kit, who jumped up and placed her white forepaws defiantly on the kitchen counter and then leveled a solemn gaze upon Rosco and Belle. The dog's black and brown muzzle was covered with white feathers; there were more stuck to the top of her head and a few pasted wetly above each eye, where they gave the impression of bushy eyebrows.

Belle gasped; she tried not to smile. "You don't suppose she's trying to emulate your Santa wig and beard, do you?"

The woof that greeted this comment was clearly one of disdain. Even the humans couldn't mistake its intent.

"I thought she'd outgrown her puppy chewing stage," Rosco observed.

"Seems more like payback time to me," was Belle's resigned response. "Maybe she's mad because Gabby had all the adventures today."

"Or perhaps she's annoyed at you for cooking up a batch of treats for another dog?"

"But I'm planning to make more for their—"

Kit interrupted by woofing briskly again; then she charged into the living room with Belle and Rosco on her heels. There, a scene of almost comical destruction greeted the humans. Feathers clung to every object as if purposely attached with glue: A lamp shade was speckled with small plumes of white; the couch and chair looked as though they were about to sprout wings; the hooked rug had an unusual downy finish; even the ceiling was daubed with snow-colored tufts.

"This can't be the result of tearing apart a single pillow," Belle said, while Rosco's sole comment was a scientific:

"Talk about a lot of static electricity. It's amazing; the feathers are almost perfectly spaced throughout the room. How'd she do that?"

Kit barked in annoyance again, then raced upstairs and flew back down again, a fresh and as yet undefiled pillow clenched in her jaws.

"Kitty, no! Bad girl! Give me that," Belle ordered, but Rosco had begun to laugh.

"I'd say you're going to need to make Kit's days a heck of a lot more entertaining when Gabby spends her time with me. Maybe the sedentary life of a crossword editor—"

"Rosco! This isn't funny!"

"Actually, it *is* pretty comical. Look at this room. It's like the inside of a chicken coop."

But Belle remained unamused. "This is a serious regression on Kit's part. Remember my beautiful red shoes—"

He corrected her. "*Shoe,* not shoes. It was only *one* red shoe. As I recall, she only liked to munch on a single piece of your footwear at a time."

Belle frowned as she removed the pillow from Kit's mouth. "I can't imagine what's gotten into her."

But Rosco was still chuckling. "Maybe she's trying to tell us she'd like a couple of little feathered pals. Is that it, Kitty? Is all this work supposed to be your idea of a message? Are you really a bird dog in disguise?"

Kit's irate and incredulous yap in response to this obviously fatuous query immediately brought Gabby, who sauntered down the stairs with her own contribution to the cause dangling from her mouth.

Belle shook her head. "And this one's taken to chewing paper . . ."

Rosco ceased his chortling in a trice. "Where did you find that, Gab?" He reached down to retrieve the wet and mangled sheet of paper, and his tone turned severe. "That's a very bad girl."

Belle glanced at the soggy mess in Rosco's hand. "She got

one of my crosswords . . . but what was she doing with it upstairs?"

Rosco balled up the paper and stuffed it in his pocket. He didn't answer his wife's question as he wracked his brain for a plausible explanation.

"In fact, where did she even *find* the puzzle? I never leave them out . . ."

"I guess you must have," Rosco mumbled. "Ahh . . . wait," he stammered. "Maybe she pulled it out of your trash can. Yeah, that's it. Then took it upstairs. She's probably had it up there for months . . . hidden under the bed."

"Are you suggesting I don't look under the bed for months on end?"

"Well, I sure don't. What's under there, anyway?"

Belle thought for a minute. "Maybe that old hallway runner that was in my dad's apartment? . . . Or?"

"See."

By now Kit and Gabby had had enough of this useless human parlay, and they embarked upon their own troubled consultation. Gabby, in full terrier mode, took the lead:

"What now, birdbrain?" she demanded of Kit. "We did everything Winston suggested, and we're in worse shape than we were before. I warned you this wasn't going to—"

"You expressed no concern with our stratagem whatsoever," Kit barked back. "It seems to me—"

"I did so. And besides, the crossword Rosco made Belle tasted disgusting! I'll be surprised if I don't get lead poisoning!"

"Pencils are made of graphite, nowadays, my dear Gabby. And for your further edification, I had to rip apart an entire pillow. And do it in the few short minutes that the humans were sequestered in the kitchen."

"It was your featherbrained idea in the first place!"

"Well, you agreed to the ploy!"

"With reservations!"

"Not that you shared with me!"

"I did, too!"

"You did not!"

"Stop it at once, you two," Belle ordered, while Rosco put his hands to his ears. Then he took his wife's hand and gave it a soothing pat:

"What do you say to a romantic fire in the fireplace, a bottle of chilled white wine—?"

"Accompanied by two yapping canines?" she rejoined.

"Doesn't *quite* rhyme with 'wine,' but you're close."

Belle grinned. "I'd say you had an excellent suggestion."

Rosco also smiled. "Good . . ."

"Vacuum up our feathered nest now or later?"

"I say let it rest. If the weather's not going to cooperate, this'll be our rendition of a white Christmas."

"And look at the bright side; it's not going to melt. Ever."

"How's about you fetching a bottle, corkscrew, and a couple of glasses, while I start the fire?"

" 'Fetch?' " Belle laughed.

"Okay, how about 'retrieve'?"

As Belle went into the kitchen, Rosco looked at Gabby. Then he pulled the sodden crossword from his pocket, smoothed it as best he could, carefully refolded it, and returned it to his pocket. "That was a naughty girl, Gabsters. You almost ruined my Christmas surprise for Belle. But not to worry; I can still read it well enough to make a copy."

Gabby whined once, which Rosco assumed was a sign of penitence, but which, in fact, was a display of complete dejection.

"Hooo boy . . ." she sighed as she curled herself into a small gray ball in front of the hearth.

"Ditto," Kit groaned while she stretched a feather-filled tummy toward the warming flames. "We're in major trouble now."

"You're darn tootin', sister."

This time, Kit didn't bother to correct the puppy's commonplace verbiage. In fact, she realized she was beginning to find such expressions rather refreshing. "Hooo boy . . ." she also sighed.

"You ain't just whistlin' Dixie, Kitty," was Gabby's muttered response. "Get ready for the invasion of the lovebirds."

"At least we're not out in the cold like that stray in the park."

"Yeah . . . mutts like that have to eat stuff with beaks and wings for breakfast."

Kit's stomach rumbled. "Yuuucchhh."

Thirteen

WHEN Stanley Hatch first saw his Secret Santa e-mail from Sara indicating that he'd "drawn" Martha Leonetti, a thud of worry banged across his chest. *Guys are so much easier,* he thought; *tie, work gloves, ski hat, belt, pen and pencil set, socks: the list goes on. A no-brainer.* Aside from Bartholomew, all the men attending the toy-wrapping party stopped into Hatch's Hardware at least once a week over the past year, eying one tool or another. If Stanley didn't know what they had their hearts set on, no one did. And if Hatch's didn't carry what a customer was yearning for, Stanley would hear about it anyway: "Man, I gotta get me a new pair of work boots," or "They say *The Sopranos* is out on DVD," or "This wallet's fallin' apart on me." For the last two months, even Rosco had been yammering about what he was yearning for. *But did he tell Belle?* Stanley wondered. *Probably not.*

But a gift for Martha? That was another story.

Ever since his wife had passed away, Stanley had taken to eating his breakfasts at Lawson's, where he enjoyed Martha's lively and often caustic sense of humor and her ability to put the grumpiest customers in their place—and even transform their sour expressions into ones of contentment. Lawson's wouldn't be the same without Martha Leonetti. But what to get her for a gift? Stanley's mind had drawn nothing but blanks, and now he found himself at the worrisome hour of ten A.M. on December twenty-third. The party at White Caps was scheduled to begin at four that afternoon. If he was going to attend, he had only six short hours in which to make his purchase. The predicament made him wonder whether he should skip the entire event. But that would leave Martha without a gift, and Stanley had a hunch she'd be far more hurt than she'd ever admit.

Leaving the hardware store to Will, his longtime assistant, Stanley walked along the sidewalk on his last-minute quest. Ace ambled beside him, sniffing the air in a lackadaisical manner. Dogs, Stanley decided, have an easy time of it during the holidays—gift-giving being totally off their radar screens. As the pair prepared to cross the street, Stan spotted Al Lever and Abe Jones at the far corner. Sensing they might be on the same mission, he turned in the opposite direction. Ace followed, and Stanley looked down and said, "One of those two probably drew me. No point in us peering over their shoulders and making their lives difficult, right, boy?"

Ace had his selective hearing set in full operational mode; he was enjoying the crisp December air too much to bother agreeing or disagreeing. *Besides,* Ace thought, *why would I care what Al Lever is up to? Does he live with a dog? Nooo . . .*

Stanley paused at each and every store window as he strolled along, all the while keeping up a running commentary which he aimed at his four-legged companion. At the pet shop, the observation was, "Huh, how about that, the love-birds are gone. Not that they were in the budget as a Secret

Santa gift . . . but I bet Martha would have liked them. But maybe, a parakeet . . . ?"

Ace snorted and shook himself. To Stanley, this translated as "Don't bet on it," and he chuckled.

"Don't think so, huh, buddy? Okay . . . birds are out." Stanley walked a few more paces down the block and stopped in front of the jewelry store, where he bent down to read a tag in the lower part of the window. "I wish they'd make it easier to see the prices from the sidewalk." He craned his neck, trying to read the numbers on a small pendant. "That looks like Martha. What do you think, boy? The green would be nice with the pink of her Lawson's uniform." He twisted his head to the other side. "Yikes!" Stanley stepped back as if the shop window had become radioactive. "Seven hundred dollars. That sure is pushing the envelope on Sara's price limit."

Next was Intimate Proposals, a lingerie shop. He rubbed his chin and said, "Hmmm . . ." while Ace barked loudly, voicing his disapproval.

"Yeah, you're right . . . too early for that sort of thing." Stanley frowned, then shook his head. " 'Too early?' Where'd that come from?"

The pair moved farther down the block and paused in front of Robertson's Stationery Supply.

"Hmmm," Stanley mused a second time. "Maybe a nice pen? Or mechanical pencil? That mother-of-pearl set is attractive, don't you think?"

Ace turned and peered up into the shop window, but offered no noticeable response.

"She's always writing down orders at work," Stanley continued. "On the other hand, it's not very personal. But then again, how well do I know her? And should I be getting her something that's personal? And what if she loses it? Customers are always borrowing waitresses' pens and not giving them back . . ."

The collie decided to lie down on the sidewalk in a warm patch of sunlight while Stanley made up his mind.

"You know, Ace, maybe it's a good thing I'm putting so much thought into this, rather than just getting her a darn poinsettia and forgetting about it. It's nice to feel something's important for a change, don't you think? What I mean is, isn't it amazing how small things like this can sneak up on you?"

Ace closed his eyes and sighed.

As Sara had promised, every name other than the two she'd targeted for her clandestine matchmaking stunt had been paired fair and square. Abe had drawn Sara herself, and Al had Belle. But unlike Stanley, who was still laboring over an appropriate Secret Santa gift, Al had yet to choose a remembrance for the most important person on his list, his wife, Helen—while Abe had a number of female "friends" he hadn't yet found "a little something" for.

"Not a problem," Abe insisted as he steered Al toward Intimate Proposals. "We can cover the whole shooting match right here: Helen, Sara, Belle, all the ladies on my list. This is where I did my thing last year; it's called, 'one-stop-last-minute-save-your-hide-shopping.' Stick with me, Al, and you're home free. And Helen will be thrilled."

Lever wasn't convinced that lingerie was the way to go for either his wife or the wife of his ex-partner, but he opted to indulge Jones. He crushed his cigarette out on the pavement outside the door, coughed twice, and said, "Whatever."

The salesclerk was in her mid-twenties, strikingly beautiful with jet-black hair and a shapely figure. She was also nearly as tall as Abe, which made her two inches taller than Al. She made no attempt to conceal the fact that she not only remembered Abe Jones from last Christmas, but also found him to be a very, *very* attractive man.

"If you need any of these items modeled, honey," she cooed, "just let me know. We're here to please."

Abe gave her one of his glowing smiles. "Why, thank you? . . . "

"Tracy."

"Tracy. That's right. How could I forget? We're just doing a little late shopping. We'll let you know if we need help."

Al's face had become bright red by this point; he tried to mask it by turning to a rack of thong panties and pretending to search for the correct size. After Tracy had moved off, he said, "I don't know, Abe, I don't think skivvies are the right choice for either Helen or Belle."

"Skivvies?" Jones pulled a filmy piece of black nylon decorated with silver beads from the rack. "Al, these are not skivvies. Boxer shorts are skivvies, not these . . . And think about it; your wife would love something sexy and alluring like this. What were you planning on getting her anyway? And please don't tell me a toaster oven."

Lever looked at him incredulously. "What do you take me for? . . . No. I thought I'd go out to the garden shop."

"What? A gardenia tree, maybe? Or a camellia? It's not bad, but not great either. We can do better."

"No, not a plant, she wanted some of those pads you put on your knees when you're pulling weeds—the green plastic ones with Velcro straps?"

Jones sighed and placed his arm over Lever's shoulder. "Look, Al, first off, she can't even use anything like that until May or June. What's she supposed to do? Stare at them yearningly and wait for the break of spring when she can at long last get down on her knees and pull some weeds out of the rhubarb patch? And second, you need to get much more personal with the women in your life. That's what they want. Here." He pulled a midnight-blue bra, panty, and garter set from the rack to his right. "What about these? Your wife will be all over you." He turned back to the rack. "Wait, hold on, they have them in red satin. Now, that's perfect for Christmas. What size is she?"

"I don't know . . . medium, I guess . . . maybe large?"

Abe rolled his eyes. "Al, Al, Al . . . You've got to come up with a *number,* here, Al. Medium or large doesn't cut it. Okay, from looking at Helen, I'm going to guess she wears a size fourteen dress. Tracy can help translate that into the correct bra measurement. Besides, if your selection doesn't fit she can always exchange it later. It's the thought that counts."

"And what thought is that?"

"Romance, Al, romance."

"I got her an electric chain saw two years back. She *loved* it."

Abe shook his head. "I'll just bet she did."

"Yeah, she doesn't have the wrist action necessary to turn over a gas model."

"I'm not even going to respond to that comment."

Lever studied the lace-edged red ensemble for what seemed like fifteen minutes. "Okay . . ." he finally sighed, "what the heck. Might as well live dangerously. But I've got to come up with something else for Belle. Rosco would string me up if I gave her an item like that."

"No pun intended?" Abe held up a pair of string panties dotted with tiny pearls and chuckled. "I think maybe I'm in the wrong section for Sara, too." He removed another pair of thong panties from a plastic hanger that weighed twice as much as the garment itself. "Not really Mrs. Briephs's color, are they? I wonder if they come in mauve or lavender?"

Lever laughed. "No, but it would be worth every penny just to see the look on her face when she opens the box."

"I value my life more than that, my friend."

"You could claim you thought it was a slingshot."

"Don't count on her believing that tale. She's as savvy as they come."

Abe went on to select a dozen sheer camisoles and panties for the women on his list. He then took them to Tracy at the sales counter.

"Well, someone's a lucky girl," she said when she saw the pile of satin, lace, and rhinestone-studded silk.

Abe cleared his throat. "Right . . . If you could just hold onto those for a minute, we're going to take a look at your body lotions."

"I recommend the Passion Fruit Massage," Tracy said as she gave Abe a slow wink. "It's one of my favorites. A real turn on, if you know what I mean."

"Yes, I believe I do."

After examining the selection of lotions, Al still wasn't convinced it was the right gift for Belle. But the product line had stimulated his imagination: *Passion Fruit, Five Berry, Tropical Milk, Wheat Germ, Avocado, Bananas and Cream.* "I think I have the perfect gift for Belle," he finally declared. "But I can't get it here."

The two men returned to the sales counter. Al made his purchase for his wife, but as Tracy wrapped the package, he fixed Abe with a level and anxious stare: "If this doesn't work, Jones, I'm holding your personally responsible."

"I'm opening a whole new world for you, Al."

"We'll see . . ."

"If Helen's not eating out of your hand Christmas morning, you can always promise her an electric drill to match that chain saw. That DeWalt yellow is very striking.

"She already has one. Cordless."

"What a guy." Abe added his gift for Sara to his other items and said, "I guess that'll be it, Tracy."

"Yes, sir. But I believe you made a slight error with the lingerie you selected."

"Really? How so?"

"They're not all the same size. Some are extra-small, some are twelves, and some are—"

"Ah, yeah, right. Um . . . I have a lot of nieces."

"Nieces? How old are they?"

". . . And a few aunts."

"Oh, that's right. I remember from last year. Yours is a very large family . . . of women."

As Al and Abe prepared to exit Intimate Proposals, Martha was just starting out on her gift-buying spree—although "spree" was not the word she would have used to describe the occasion. Unwillingness to enter into the spirit of the season made her drag her feet in a manner that was decidedly inconsistent with her normal efficiency. *Bah, humbug,* she grumbled to herself. *Who cares about this Secret Santa stuff anyway? The holiday's for kids, isn't it? So let's just wrap the tots' gifts and call it a day. I don't need a fancy party at Sara's house. And I don't need to be buying—or making—something for a person I hardly know. I mean, of all the weird luck! Why couldn't I have drawn Belle for my Secret Santa? Or Rosco or Bartholomew or even Abe or Al? Why Stanley Hatch? We're no more than passing acquaintances . . . and what do you choose for a widower? Joke gifts are out, right?*

But here was Martha's true dilemma. She did know Stanley. Not only was he a sometime member of the "canine corps," he'd also been a daily customer at Lawson's since his wife's death. He was a good and decent guy—who, unfortunately, was currently available, which only made matters worse. Cowardice, especially cowardice in dealing with male customers, was not an emotion Martha relished.

"Darn!" she muttered aloud. "Darn!" For the fourth time in as many minutes, she considered avoiding the entire event. But instead, she plodded along and finally drifted into the sporting goods shop. But there, everything looked either too impersonal or just the opposite. *I can't get him a hat,* she told herself, *or gloves or a fleece scarf. Who doesn't own plenty of warm gear like that in New England?* She picked up and rejected a mini-flashlight, a canteen, a set of camping dinnerware, a book with detailed maps of local hikes, and a utensil that served as spoon, fork, and knife all together. *He may not even like camping,* she decided. *I know I don't. And you can just forget about climbing along any mountain trail.*

She walked grimly back to the street, turned the corner, and started again. *The antique shop? The new cooking emporium? A gift from the pet store to share with Ace?* Then she spotted Fennimore's Bookshop, and a light bulb went off in her head.

IT was three minutes after Martha had vanished into the bookshop's wooden stacks that Al Lever's beeper buzzed him. He handed Abe the gilded bag that contained Helen's present, and the paper sack that contained Belle's gift, then punched numbers into his cell phone.

"Lever. What's up?" he stated, although anyone at NPD would have recognized Al's voice before he reached the first "e."

"The Staties just picked up two of their guys, Al," the voice reported.

"Only two?"

"What they said."

"Meaning one's still out there."

"Affirmative. The two clowns aren't talking either, so there's no telling where the third's got himself to."

"Which one's still loose?"

"Scraggs, the faa . . . er, heavyset one. The Staties also said they'd reclaimed *most* of the stolen weapons."

"Most?"

"That's a direct quote. No additional information supplied. Men of few words, those Staties."

Lever signed off and looked at Abe. "We've still got one armed Santa on the loose."

"A one-armed Santa? Must be tough handling those eight reindeer."

"You slay me, Abe."

"Don't go there, Al. You want a one-armed Santa and a *sleigh,* you got it."

"I'll stick with 'slay.' Which may be my fate when Helen gets a load of the gift you've talked me into."

Fourteen

WHITE Caps was decorated for the season as it always had been. What had been considered festive in Sara's parents' day—and probably her grandparents' and great grandparents' before them—she deemed appropriate now. Christmas, or indeed any holiday, she felt should be accorded the tradition it deserved. Thus, the ten-foot-tall balsam fir in the sitting room, the swags of white pine bedecking the main stairs, the cedar garlands draping each fireplace mantle, the *cache pots* of fragrant paper-white narcissus dotting every polished mahogany tabletop. Sara's conservatory was a busy place in the weeks leading up to this important event—just as it had been in years gone by.

"Welcome, welcome," she beamed as her guests arrived—another longstanding custom being that the mistress of the house be the first to greet her guests rather than have the door opened by Emma, the parlor maid who'd been in Sara's employ for more than forty years.

"We have refreshments set out in both the sitting room

and dining room; the children's gifts to be wrapped are arranged there, as well. There were so many presents that Emma and I chose to divide them up; otherwise the task of affixing paper and ribbon to each and every item seemed rather daunting. But I'm asking that our own Secret Santa gifts be placed on the sideboard in the dining room. We can open our offerings to one another following our light collation." Sara gave Belle an almost imperceptible wink, while Al, who'd just arrived with Helen, said:

"And what's your idea of a 'light collation,' Mrs. B.?" Al was the only person who got away with calling Sara "Mrs. B." just as she was the only human on earth who was permitted to refer to him as "Albert."

"Emma and I decided upon a smoked turkey breast to accompany the traditional oyster stew, Albert dear. Deviled eggs for Belle, of course, and a caviar mousse, which also will serve as an *hors d'oeuvre*. Then a Welsh rarebit, because my father always insisted upon it, an escallop of leeks and potatoes, a hot vegetable terrine, a green salad . . . oh, and a mincemeat pie with hard sauce for dessert. One simply cannot celebrate Christmas without hard sauce!"

"That doesn't sound like a 'light' anything, Mrs. B—especially a sauce made almost entirely of butter. I'm trying to watch my weight, you know." Al patted his stomach, a gesture that made Abe Jones roll his eyes.

"You're lovely just the way you are, Albert," was Sara's lofty reply.

Rosco mouthed the word *lovely* as Al gave him a superior nod. A short moment later, Bartholomew arrived, and on his heels Martha and Stanley, who entered the foyer in an unexpected and nervous hush.

"Martha, my dear!!" Sara said, giving her an expansive hug. "I'm so glad you could make it! Your friends need you every bit as much as your niece does. Oh, and here's your gift to add to the Secret Santa horde; and yours, too, Stan and Bartholomew. It looks very much like an article of gentleman's hosiery might be hiding in that box you're bearing. Well, let's get to the business at hand, and then we can reward ourselves with a meal and our gift exchange. There's eggnog for those who wish it, or mulled cider for those among us who feel an obligation to watch their calories. I do not refer to you, of course, Albert."

This year, it was Abe who proved the most deft at wrapping the gathered toys. Not only was he speedier than the others, he was also a whiz at creating complicated, curling, and multi-layered bows.

"Either you're getting domesticated, Abe," Al observed, "or you've got far too much time to play around with sharp instruments."

"Can't a guy have a 'soft' side, Al?" Abe rejoined while Helen observed a pithy:

"Appreciating the prettier things in life wouldn't kill you, Al."

"That's just what I was telling your hubby just this morning, Helen. Women like to see a guy's sensitive side every now and then."

"I take it that he didn't listen," she replied. Her tone was dry but loving, and she gave her husband a quick, indulgent smile.

Abe shrugged. "Hey, you married him. You know what a hard case the guy is."

"Thank you for your input, Mister Helpful," Al remarked.

THERE were so many gilt-edged plates on the dining room table, it was nearly impossible to see the damask cloth covering its surface. Sara's rule for this "light collation" was that the meal be treated with childlike abandon. The courses could be enjoyed in succession or eaten at the same time—or even indulged in reverse order. So bowls of creamy oyster stew sat beside pie plates which in turn sat next to dinner platters heaped with smoked turkey and escalloped leeks and vegetable terrine. There was eggnog in crystal punch cups, cutglass pitchers of warmed mulled cider, and champagne in delicate flutes. Above all, there was joy and the occasional spontaneous singing of Christmas carols.

"I'm going to begin with my gift to Albert," Sara announced at last. "And then we can go around the table clockwise." She walked to the sideboard and retrieved a shallow, rectangular box. "You have to guess."

Al gently shook the present. "Cigars," he said. "It's an educated guess." He smiled at her. "I can smell them." He opened the package, and then stared at Sara in wonderment. "These are Cuban . . . the real deal. How did you—?"

"You forget, Albert, that my brother's a U.S. senator. I'd prefer not to go into too many details, so I suggest you simply enjoy them."

Al gazed at the cigars and then looked back at Sara. "But these must have cost a fortune, Mrs. B. I thought we'd agreed that our gifts should be reasonably priced—"

"I am an old lady, Albert, a very *rich* old lady who has, alas, no direct heirs. If my gift embarrasses you, I apologize, but since I can't take it with me, I feel it's only fitting that I treat my friends as I would family. Indeed, in the years since my son died, all of you at this table have become as close as family. Closer, perhaps. One can never choose one's relatives. True friendships are another thing. They require what I refer to as the 'acid test'—which in my case can be a tart tongue and a critical eye. I still wince when I remember how I treated our

Belle when I first met her. Although, I think she's forgiven me." Sara smiled at Belle, who beamed in return. "She's become the granddaughter I never had." Then, with customary asperity—the mistress of White Caps didn't believe in 'overindulging emotions'—she turned to Bartholomew, who was seated to her left. "Your turn."

As Sara had guessed, his offering was "gentleman's hosiery," in this case a pair of red socks for Rosco. They were embroidered with smiling Santas and green holly leaves.

"I know you eschew any woolly footwear, dear boy," Bartholomew stated. "But I couldn't resist. It was the jolly faces of Father Christmas festooning them that attracted me. I hope they'll become a memento of the year our local Saint Nicks were nearly carted off to the hoosegow by the Massachusetts constabulary.

Belle then walked to the sideboard and presented Bartholomew with the tin of homemade biscuits, and the gift rendered Newcastle's normally verbose gossip columnist speechless as he seemed consumed by a wave of emotion. "And you baked them yourself!" he finally managed to murmur. "I can't recall anyone *making* something for me. How very, very kind. I've never . . . I've never . . . and what a clever shape . . . Bones for the 'cur'—" Words again failed him. He pulled out a voluminous linen handkerchief and wiped tears from his eyes, and Belle couldn't decide whether to bend down and give the little man a hug or to pretend he hadn't lost his composure.

It was Sara who saved the day. "There there, Bartholomew. You and I are becoming two peas out of the same pod. We'll be crying into our soup soon if we don't take care."

"It's just that . . ." Bartholomew gulped noisily.

"I understand. The season produces strong sentiments. But I believe we're better off reacting to whatever stirs our souls rather than turning our heads and hardening our hearts. My grandmother—if you can believe such an ancient person existed—used to tell me that the greatest of emotions was courage. Because without it, we can experience no other to its fullest . . ."

As Sara spoke, Martha stared at the plates in front of her; her cheeks were flushed a bright and anxious pink.

"I suppose," Kerr said as he wiped a final tear from his eye, "that it would be polite to pass them around?" He handed the tin to Rosco. "Although I'm sure you've already sampled them."

Rosco choked back his laughter, then glanced at his wife, who looked both mortified and worried that her gift might inadvertently cause Bartholomew pain.

"Actually, Belle made them for Winston," Rosco said quietly. "That's why they're shaped like bones."

"But they're peanut butter and banana," Belle chimed in. "And the ingredients are all natural. I guess people could eat them . . . Rosco, why don't you try one and see how they taste?"

"Ahhh . . ."

"I won't hear of it," Bartholomew said with a grand gesture, retrieving the tin from Rosco. "Winston will be twenty pounds heavier before the New Year but contented, nonetheless. His thank you note shall be posted in the morning."

"Now you, Albert," Sara voiced after additional laughter had subsided. Everyone watched as Al presented Belle with a cookbook, which suddenly caused him to stammer in embarrassment.

"It's for making jams and jellies and fruit desserts and stuff like that. Not that I don't think you're good at . . . well, you know what I mean. Because we all know you're an egghead, and—"

"No pun intended," Abe Jones interrupted.

Al gave him a look. "Mister Helpful rides to the rescue once again."

But Belle was already laughing. "And you couldn't find a copy of *Culinary Clues for Nincompoops?*"

"No, Belle, really, I . . . what I mean is—"

"Sit down before your foot completely disappears into your mouth, Al," Helen chortled as Belle responded with a genuinely grateful:

"This is terrific, Al, really. Yesterday, dog biscuits, tomorrow . . ." She began flipping through the recipes. ". . . fruit whips!"

"They're not for, like, animal training, are they?" Al asked.

"No," Belle chuckled, "they're for people, and they sound divine."

After that, Abe gave Sara a bottle of Passion Fruit Body Rub which promised to be "the elixir of romance."

"Perhaps you failed to hear me mention the fact that I'm an old lady, Dr. Jones," Sara teased, to which Abe's reply was a smooth:

"You're as young as you want to be, Sara. Anyway, women only grow better with time. That came highly recommended by the salesgirl."

"I can only imagine. I've walked by the shop; I can guess she has a few whips of her own stored away."

The gift exchange continued around the table, but just as Stanley and Martha were poised to reach for their gifts, an eruption of loud and angry barking intruded.

"Whatever can that be?" Sara asked. "Neither of my adjacent neighbors has a dog . . ." She listened more intently. "The sound seems to be coming from the conservatory. Goodness, that's an excited creature. You'll have to excuse me, but I think some investigation is in order."

Sara pushed back her chair, but Al was already on his feet. "You're not going outside, Mrs. B."

"I most certainly am, Albert. I'm not going to remain idly indoors while some poor creature may be trapped in my—"

"Rosco and I can handle it. There's no point in breaking up your nice party." The two men exchanged a glance, then Al looked at Abe Jones. "Alert NPD, will ya? Tell them something's 'trapped' in Mrs. B's greenhouse. We may need some backup over here."

Fifteen

AL and Rosco could hear the hostile shouts of a man cursing a blue streak before they were halfway to Sara's conservatory. The oaths were mingled with equally angry snarls that sounded as though they were produced by an enraged mountain lion rather than a dog. The ferocious cacophony was at odds with the delicate two-story Victorian glass structure that glowed palely but serenely in the cold, dark night: a place of hothouse roses and geraniums "wintering over," of orchids housed in a special wing, and ancient gardenia trees surrounding a pleasant rotunda. Coarse language and yelping bays had no home there.

"Are you thinking what I'm thinking, Poly—crates?" Al asked under his breath.

" 'Fraid so, Al. But then again, it could be just a vagrant who broke in . . ." Rosco's tone was equally tense and hushed. "There's a couple of them around town with dogs—"

"Not animals that want to kill them."

"True. But our cons didn't have a dog—"

"Change of disguise . . . ya get yourself a new accessory."

"And hope that it doesn't bite your head off?"

The two walked on, more carefully now. Both had their weapons drawn.

"Mrs. B. would have a cow if her prize what-do-ya-call-'em got wrecked," Al said under his breath.

"Dendrobiums?"

"Yeah, something like that."

"I think she'd understand, 'Albert.' "

"Well, if there's any mishaps, I can always pin the blame on you."

"You've got such a big heart, my friend."

The pair approached the building's corner, further slowing their pace, then slipped soundlessly through a half-open door. Between the colonnade of pillars supporting the arched roof, they could see a large man at the far end of the structure. He stood in profile, his back against an empty potting table; in his right hand was a revolver with which he flailed unsuccessfully at a large, shaggy yellow dog who repeatedly leapt toward him with swift and fearless lunges; the shredded sleeves of the man's jacket indicated that the animal's teeth had already connected more than once.

"What do we have here?" Al muttered. "Sure looks like 'Santa' Scraggs to me."

"Having problems with his reindeer, though," was Rosco's quick reply.

"Yup. Seems like he and 'Rudolph' are up to their eyeballs in a bit of a disagreement."

"Probably not a sled dog."

Al and Rosco moved into a low, crouching position, then raised their weapons, leveling them in Scraggs' direction. The yellow dog turned, suddenly aware of company, while Scraggs took advantage of this momentary respite.

"Call off your pit bull or he's dead meat," he yelled. He pointed his large revolver directly at the dog, but the animal spun back toward him, hurtling into Scraggs's hip, and throwing him momentarily off balance. Righting himself, the escaped prisoner lashed out with his left foot, landing a fierce kick that caught the big dog under the chest and sent it spiraling backwards across the stone floor. But the animal recovered quickly and resumed its determined and even more aggressive attack, snarling louder and jumping higher. This time its teeth latched onto the hand holding the .357.

"Friggin' mutt!" the man screamed in pain. "I told you to call him off!" Scraggs tried to take aim again, but the pistol was already starting to slip from his bleeding fingers. "Friggin' mutt! Who puts an attack dog in a friggin' greenhouse? What are you bozos growin' in here anyways, marijuana?"

"Just hold it right where you are, fella. I'm a police officer," was Lever's cool reply. He removed his detective's shield from his belt, and held it high in his left hand. The dim light gave the badge a greenish luster.

"You're under arrest," Lever continued. "Now, put your weapon down. Nice and slow. You move too quick, it'll be the last move you make. In case you haven't noticed, my four-legged buddy here doesn't like quick movements . . . and neither do I."

"Friggin' cops. What did you do, leave wild dogs in empty buildings all over the friggin' city? This is the second time I ran into the damn thing—"

The yellow dog barked noisily, then embarked on a deep and rumbling growl that forced Scraggs to shiver slightly.

"Friggin' mutt! Hidin' under a damn . . . I woulda shot it right off, except for I didn't want the noise to . . . If I'd nailed the thing at that coffee shop yesterday morning—"

"Drop your weapon, Scraggs," Lever repeated. "Nice and easy."

Scraggs considered his options for a long moment while his eyes darted from the dog's exposed teeth to Lever's and Rosco's weapons and back to the dog. Eventually the .357 clattered to the floor, but Al and Rosco hesitated before moving forward to cuff the prisoner.

"We better call animal control—" Al began when the yellow dog suddenly abandoned its threatening stance. In fact, it seemed to lose interest in Scraggs altogether, and instead trotted to Al's side where it sat and gave one hearty bark as if to say, "He's all yours." Then it leaned its wide head against Lever's thigh and thumped its heavy tail against the floor.

"I'll be darned," Al muttered. "If that face doesn't look exactly like Skippy's—"

"Skippy?" Rosco glanced at Lever, but Al's response was soft and incredulous. "Good boy. You're a good boy . . . Skip . . ."

"Cops and their friggin' werewolves," Scraggs snarled as Rosco removed the handcuffs from Lever's belt and attached them to the fugitive's wrists. Lever said nothing. He continued to gaze in wonderment at the dog, who now seemed unwilling to leave his side. Whatever emotion human and canine were experiencing, it appeared to be mutual.

With Scraggs in police custody, Rosco, Al, and "Skippy Two" returned to Sara's house. Only twenty minutes or so had elapsed since the escaped convict's rearrest, but the yellow dog and Lever had already started to bond. "A little thin, aren't you, boy?" Al almost cooed. "We'll have to get you some grub, but not to worry, Mrs. B.'s sure to have loads of leftovers. You like smoked turkey?"

Rosco had never heard his former partner use such an affectionate tone, even with Helen. "Who was Skippy One?" he finally asked.

Al's reply was a husky-voiced "Dog I had as a kid. We had to move. The new place my folks found didn't take pets." He shrugged. "It was a rental. So . . . so, some lucky person got himself a real nice pooch. Skip could do every trick in the book . . ." Al concealed his emotion by bending down to stroke "Skippy Two" 's tattered ears. ". . . And I bet you can, too, can't you, boy? . . ." Lever continued to rub the dog's sooty head. Both man and dog seemed utterly transformed. "Look, Poly—crates, you go on in and get back to the party. I'm going to take my man, Skip, to the back door. He needs some serious chow . . . Besides, this tail could wreck more than a few pricey things in that sitting room. Heck, I feel like a bull in a china shop in there myself."

Rosco didn't consider it wise to mention that "Skippy Two" might not be invited to join the party in his present state. Instead he retorted with, "Too bad your Secret Santa didn't give you a leash. There's a law, you know?" But the jest was lost on Al. It was doubtful he even heard it. "Any message you want me to pass along to Helen?" he added, but that seemed to fall on deaf ears, as well. "Your wife?"

Rosco returned to the party. "Your hubby's got himself a new best friend," he told Helen. "But I'd suggest you give him a bath before inviting him to share your bed. On the other hand, you may not have much choice." Rosco looked at Martha. "The guy you most enjoy poking with a fork has turned into a Mr. Softie . . ." But something in her expression made the joke die before Rosco finished it. She looked like a deer caught in a pair of headlights.

"Martha and Stan are about to exchange their Secret Santa gifts," Belle explained in a voice Rosco thought was a little too bright and eager to please. "They drew *each other* as partners. Isn't that a *coincidence?*"

Stanley seemed more comfortable with this fact than Martha. He held out a small rectangular box; Martha's gift was clenched in fingers that hung at her side. For a moment Rosco wished mightily that Sara hadn't arranged the "coincidence."

"You know," Stan said, "I wasn't happy I'd drawn Martha at first . . . no offense, Martha . . . but I thought, well, a guy . . . I know what to get a guy. That would have been easy. Hunting up something for Martha was hard—which was actually a good thing . . ." He seemed about to continue, but instead thrust the package into her empty hand. "I hope you like it."

Martha put down her own gift as she opened Stanley's. Inside was a handkerchief, the fabric so sheer as to be almost translucent, and the lace border wide and delicate and ruffled. "Oh!" she gasped, "How did you know?"

"I got it in the new antique shop. It's got an M on it . . . in pink, like your Lawson's outfit. I realize it's a little frilly, but I thought that if you didn't like it you could always—"

"But I *collect* handkerchiefs," Martha blurted out. "I especially like antique ones! Oh, look at the M! Oh, it's beautiful!" She held up her gift while Sara gave Belle a furtive and knowing glance.

"And what did you get Stanley, dear?"

"A book . . . Oh, no! I didn't mean to say that . . . Here." Martha thrust her present into Stan's hands. "Forget you heard me . . ."

Stan opened the wrapping. "Rudyard Kipling's poetry . . ."

Martha winced. "I just . . . I mean . . . I didn't—"

"My granddad used to quote from *If* all the time," Stan interrupted. There was a genuine smile on his face. "I haven't heard it since the old man passed on . . ." He began flipping through pages. "Here. This is the passage:

'If you can force your heart and nerve and sinew

To serve your turn long after they are gone,

And so hold on when there is nothing in you

Except the Will which says to them: 'Hold On!' . . ."

He looked at the gathered company and finally at Martha. "Thank you," he said. "Thank you very, very much." His eyes had misted up. Rosco was happy Al wasn't there to witness the spectacle, but then he realized Al's—and Skippy Two's—eyes were probably just as dreamy and damp.

Sixteen

"I hope you're pleased with yourself . . . You and Sara, both." It was late Christmas eve, and Rosco and Belle were tucked into bed, while Kit and Gabby were ensconced in their own pillowy nests on the floor. The dogs were only half-awake as they listened to the drone of human speech; vigilance, for the moment, had been placed on the back burner.

"Well, didn't it work out perfectly? Stan and Martha couldn't have found more ideal gifts for one another. And the way they were looking at each other? Sara thinks—"

"I know *exactly* what she thinks," Rosco chortled. "But not even Sara Crane Briephs can arrange marriage proposals nowadays."

"No one mentioned anything like that, Rosco!"

"Sara did." He laughed again. "In this very house, in fact."

"I think it's terrific what happened," Belle retorted with a smug smile. "Even if Stan and Martha simply become better friends."

"Mmmm hmmm . . . And since Sara's the Newcastle big-wig in charge of the random drawing to determine who wins the *Crier*'s puzzle contest this year—"

"She'd never *fix* a contest!" Belle insisted.

"Oh, no?" Rosco chuckled.

"I'm certain she wouldn't. I'm *pretty* certain she wouldn't . . ."

"Unless Stanley or Martha are among the contestants . . ." Rosco shook his head while Belle frowned:

"Sara *wouldn't* . . . would she?"

Rosco grinned. "Well, I hope she realizes she's going to needs to arrange a better companion for Helen ASAP."

"What's wrong with Al?"

"Did you see him when we left the party? I was surprised he even remembered Helen was with him. He opened the door for the new Skippy—who very nearly got to ride shotgun. If Helen doesn't watch her step she may be relegated to the backseat on all family outings."

Belle sighed happily. "The bigger they are, the harder they fall."

"I wouldn't use those precise words with our 'Albert,' if I were you."

"I didn't know he'd had a dog when he was a kid. I didn't think he even *liked* animals."

"He had me fooled." Rosco shrugged, then put his arm around his wife; and she cuddled against him while a prolonged groan rose from the floor.

"I think we're being told it's too late for any hanky-panky, Rosco."

"Since when do our four-legged pals make the decisions around here?"

"I hope you don't expect an honest response to a loopy

question like that." Belle stretched away to turn out the light, then stopped mid-movement. "Okay, so what did you get me for Christmas?"

"Aren't you jumping the gun a little?"

"It's eleven-thirty . . . No, it's eleven-thirty-three, almost thirty-four . . ." She leapt out of bed. "I'll go first."

Whether it was Belle's feet hitting the floor or the recognition that the ominous gift exchange was finally upon them, both dogs became fully alert in an instant. They looked at each other, their ears cocked to full listening mode, their brains concentrating on feathers and twittering songs.

"It's a crossword," Belle said, sliding back between the covers. "You have to fill in the answers to learn what your gift is. I brought you a pen."

"Why don't you just read me the answers. If it's anything like your *Belle's Nöel*, it might be Independence Day before I figure this thing out."

"Spoilsport."

Rosco grinned and sat up straighter. Then he pulled open the drawer in his bedside table. "I made you a puzzle, too. Actually, I had help—"

"From who?"

"Isn't it *whom?*"

"Don't split hairs. Who was it?"

"The same person who helped me with the puzzle I used as a marriage proposal. And good detectives never reveal private sources."

"It was Sara, wasn't it? And she didn't breathe a word. Not even when we discussed her role in the competition."

"Detectives never reveal private sources, Belle—"

"And Al probably, too. That's so unfair, Rosco! Everyone's in on the secret except me!"

Both Gabby and Kit woofed in unison.

"Well, except for those two four-legged loafers." Belle laughed. "Because I doubt your clandestine constructors were of the canine variety . . . Wait! Was it *your* puzzle that Gab was chewing on the other day? I thought something seemed fishy about the way you acted when you snatched it from her mouth . . ." But Belle's words trailed off as she began hurriedly writing in puzzle clues. "Oh, Rosco! You constructed a poem. How clever—and sweet . . ."

"It's more doggerel than poetry, I'm afraid. But it rhymes, if you use your imagination."

"*Dog*-what?" Belle was so engrossed in the crossword she scarcely heard her husband.

"Never mind."

"No . . . what did you say? Something about a dog?"

Rosco laughed and looked over her shoulder. "Hey, that's not fair! You can't just fill in the HER GIFT part. You have to work the Down clues, too." He pulled the crossword from her hand.

"Give me that!"

"My turn to learn what *my* gift is . . . But you'll have to be patient. I'm a lot slower at these cryptic word diversions than you . . ."

Gabby and Kit began to whine in frustration.

"Do you think they're asking to go out again?" Belle wondered.

"I think they're *telling* us to shut up and go to sleep so we're bright-eyed and bushy-tailed for Santa's gift deliveries tomorrow morning," was Rosco's amused reply.

Out of sight of the humans, Gabby hung her head in disbelief, while Kit, who previously would have deemed this behavior unnecessarily corny and theatrical, decided it was just the ticket. Stoic New Englanders, she thought, could learn a lot from their thespian counterparts in southern California.

"This could take all night," Gabby whimpered.

"You said it," Kit grumbled in response, while Belle kept up a running description of the crossword she'd created for Rosco.

". . . I wrote a poem, too . . . It's really an I.O.U. because you'll have to try—"

"Hey, don't tell me!"

"You're right. I'm not going to say another word. But then we haven't had any snow or even a good, solid freeze—"

"You have no self-control whatsoever. Have I ever told you that?"

"About a million times. It's just that I'm not certain a pair of—" She clapped her hand over her mouth. "That's it! I'm not saying another word, I swear."

Rosco gave her a kiss. "You're as bad as Martha."

"It's not a book, if that's what you're thinking," Belle insisted.

"I gathered that much. Now, are you going to *tell* me what my present is or let me figure it out on my own?"

"My lips are sealed," Belle answered with a grin. "Why don't we *both* fill in our crosswords at the same time—bearing in mind that I've already supplied you with a major, and I mean *major*, clue."

"This isn't a competion, Belle."

"Oh, no? . . . On your mark, get set, go!"

This was too much suspense for Kit and Gabby, who simultaneously jumped on the bed and began pouncing up and down.

"What's gotten into you, Kit?" Belle demanded. "I thought you'd outgrown these puppy antics. And, you, Gab; you're supposed to be learning ladylike behaviour from your 'big sister'. . . ." But Belle's heart wasn't in this reprimand, because even as she spoke her eyes were scanning the cross-word Rosco had given her.

"Oh, Rosco!" she burst out. "ONE PAIR OF LOVELY . . . Oh, what an extravagant, wonderful gift! I saw them in the shop window, and I . . . and I—" She threw her arms around her husband's neck. "Oh, thank you! Thank you! Thank you!"

Gabby looked at Kit, who stared levelly at her in return. "One pair of *lovely* . . . ?" rumbled from the bigger dog's throat. "One pair of *lovely* . . . ? And you let us get completely bamboozled into thinking . . . ? And all the work I went through? All that chewing and shredding?"

"That's what I heard him say. Honest! I mean, I thought that's what he . . . Because a 'pair of love' and a 'pair of *lovely*': they're almost the same thing, aren't they?"

"Someone's got to teach you the difference between adjectives and adverbs, young Gabby. Or in this instance, adjectives and nouns—"

But Gabby yipped Kit into silence. "Look! Look out the window! What are those white spots flying around?"

Kit turned her head. "Snow, you birdbrain."

"My first snowfall." Gabby's terrier voice had turned docile and full of awe.

Then Kit also began to stare through the window, and the stillness of both dogs caused Belle and Rosco to take notice, too. "The first snow of the year," they said almost in unison, while Belle curled up close to Rosco and added a soft:

"I guess it's going to be cold enough for my gift after all."

ACROSS

1. Hit-run link
4. Payroll info
7. Explosive letters
10. Not many
13. Map abbr.
14. Also
15. "The ___ to a man's heart . . ."
16. Mellow
17. HER GIFT, part 1
21. Classic roadster
22. *Sunset Boulevard* Oscar nominee
23. Letter opener?
26. CCCX ÷ II
27. Passion
31. HER GIFT, part 2
35. Amish possessive
36. "___ Day Now"
37. Add fizz
38. Broccoli ___
40. Greek nine
41. "Excellent!"
44. "Sounds new to me?"
45. "The ___ Side"
48. HER GIFT, part 3
52. Mets' home
53. VCR setting
54. The Good Book
55. Machinations
58. Served Kit & Gabby
59. HER GIFT, part 4
66. Goof
67. Hawaiian wreath
68. Inc. leader
69. Yours and mine
70. Airport posting
71. Bruin battleground
72. Perfect Olympic score
73. Old Pontiac

DOWN

1. Mr. Garfunkel
2. ___ degree
3. Joey ___ & the Starliters
4. Reputation stain
5. Davenport
6. "___ a creature was . . ."
7. "The ___ Days of Christmas"
8. Collars
9. Rookie
10. Fenway Park attendee
11. With 63-Down, holiday quaff
12. Director Craven
18. Caddy financer
19. Hunter or tree
20. How to pay for a Ferrari?
23. Wrestling spot
24. Bat material
25. *Lover Come Back* star
26. Pine adornment
28. Italian one
29. Cpl's next step
30. Literary monogram
32. Synagogue leader
33. *Eating* ___
34. Ready-go link
38. Fix
39. Mr. Parseghian
40. Data; abbr.
41. May-day
42. Durham campus; abbr.
43. ___ Dee River, S.C.
44. Classic Christmas dinner
45. Valentine mo.
46. "___ I want for Christmas . . ."

🌴 *Rosco's Gift To Belle* 🌴

47. *Catcher in the* ___
49. Tour stagehand
50. King of the fairies
51. Veni-vici link
56. Artist Salvador
57. Util. bill
58. Certain sports agent?
59. Wide shoe
60. A-Team member

61. Pitcher's stat.
62. Do something
63. See 11-Down
64. Some tennis strings
65. Sign of a hit

ACROSS

1. Brainy numbers; abbr.
4. Back of the boat
7. NYC subway line
10. Not LG
13. Fruitcake?
14. Reel partner
15. Classic car
16. Foot digit
17. HIS GIFT, part 1
21. Update
22. Not quite due?
23. Mr. Estrada
24. HIS GIFT, part 2
27. "Wait a ___ !"
28. Fair grade
29. "___ girl!"
33. Toss in
35. Caesar and Waldorf
40. Santa Claus across The Pond
43. Confederate general
44. Fall back
45. "___ Be Cruel"
46. Cheat
48. News network; abbr.
50. HIS GIFT, part 3
59. Couple
60. Orr field?
61. Best results
62. HIS GIFT, part 4
65. Kingston campus; abbr.
66. Tiny
67. Volta feeder
68. Picnic pest
69. Ethnic of Laos
70. Hippie drug
71. 2-Down's org.
72. Draft org.

DOWN

1. Lemur
2. Bogart role
3. Italian subdivision
4. Cupid's barbs
5. Valentine's candy?
6. Pat 6-pointers
7. Curiously opposite
8. Directional notices at the North Pole?
9. Gift for a tot
10. Baby's first ride?
11. Film
12. Tall onions
18. Decay
19. "Stop the shot!"
20. Grassland
25. Power options; abbr.
26. Green, black & Earl Grey
29. "No ___ , ands or buts."
30. Make lace
31. RV hookup?
32. "Gotcha!"
34. UPS rival
36. Ford model
37. Latin love
38. Dapper ___
39. Retired flyer; abbr.
41. Therefore
42. Steamy
47. Hen ___
49. Table cloth?
50. Pipe drug
51. Mother-of-pearl
52. Old McDonald refrain
53. Scientology monogram
54. Confederate general
55. "Give ___ rest."

🌴 Belle's Gift to Rosco 🌴

56. Namesakes of a meter maid
57. Signs
58. Skips lunch
63. Wise one
64. "I Only Have Eyes for ___ "

The Answers

🌴 Belle's Nöel 🌴

1 H	2 A	3 D	4 J		5 M	6 A	7 T	8 T		9 R	10 O	11 S	12 A
13 A	T	O	I		14 S	A	I	O	R	15 U	P	O	N
16 T	E	E	N		17 P	U	M	P	U	D	18 D	I	N	G
		19 G	20 O	O	D	S		21 R	O	N		
22 A	23 P	24 P	E	P	I	E		25 C	A	P	I	T	O	26	27 O
28 N	I	B	B	E	S		29 H	O	Y	H	O	C	K
30 D	E	A	E	R		31 H	I	M		32 N	U	S
	33 S	A	34 N	35 T	A	C	A	36 U	37 S	
38 A	39 M	40 F		41 E	I	S		42 N	E	A	43 T	44 O	45
46 X	M	A	47 S	48 B	A	S		49 I	F	I	C	A	N
50 E	A	S	H	E	S		51 W	A	I	G	H	T	S
	52 H	I	E		53 F	A	I	T	H	
54 E	55 A	P	I	N	G		56 G	57 O	R	D	S		58 B	59 A	60 R	61 N
62 F	R	A	N		63 E	R	O	D	E		64 E	V	E	N
65 T	A	N	G		66 T	O	M	E		67 S	A	V	E

🌴 If Dogs Made Crosswords 🌴

¹G	²R	³R	■	⁴A	⁵P	⁶E	■	■	⁷S	⁸N	⁹I ¹⁰F ¹¹F
¹²R A E			■	¹³R	¹⁴U I N		■	¹⁵P	E O R I A		
¹⁶A B C			■	¹⁷S	P E E		■	¹⁸R	A I S E D		
¹⁹T	B	O	²⁰N	E	P	I	C	²¹K	E N S	■	■
²²A I D A			■	²³Y	O K E		■	²⁴E	²⁵B ²⁶R ²⁷O		
■	²⁸T	E	S	²⁹L	A	■	³⁰A	³¹B ³²E	³³A C E		
■	³⁴A	I	M		■	³⁵O	N Y X		³⁶R A D		
■	³⁷B	³⁸E	L	M	O	³⁹N	T S T E	⁴⁰A	K S	■	
⁴¹H O G			■	⁴²P	R O S		■	⁴³H	R H		
⁴⁴A N G			■	⁴⁵S	E A		■	⁴⁶E	T H E ⁴⁷R	⁴⁸R	
⁴⁹M E S S		⁵⁰S	■	⁵¹R	⁵²A ⁵³S P		■	⁵⁴A	D E S	⁵⁵S	
■	⁵⁶P	⁵⁷O	⁵⁸R	K	C H O P	⁵⁹H	I L L				
⁶⁰C	⁶¹A	⁶²M	E R A	■	⁶³T	R U E	■	⁶⁴B	O O		
⁶⁵B R E A T H				■	⁶⁶S	E N T	■	⁶⁷L	A P		
⁶⁸S I L K S				■	■	⁶⁹D	D E	⁷⁰E	D S		

🌴 Rosco's Gift To Belle 🌴

1 A	2 N	3 D		4 S	5 S	6 N		7 T	8 N	9 T		10 F	11 E	12 W
13 R	T	E		14 T	O	O		15 W	A	Y		16 A	G	E
17 T	H	E	18 G	I	F	T	19 H	E	B	R	20 I	N	G	S
			21 M	G	A		22 O	L	S	O	N			
23 M	24 A	25 D	A	M		26 C	L	V			27 L	28 U	29 S	30 T
31 A	S	A	C	A	32 R	O	L	E	33 R	34 S	I	N	G	S
35 T	H	Y			36 A	N	Y		37 A	E	R	A	T	E
			38 R	39 A	B	E		40 I	O	T	A			
41 S	42 U	43 P	E	R	B		44 G	N	U			45 F	46 A	47 R
48 O	N	E	P	A	I	49 R	O	F	L	50 O	51 V	E	L	Y
52 S	H	E	A			53 O	O	O		54 B	I	B	L	E
			55 I	56 D	57 E	A	S		58 F	E	D			
59 E	60 M	61 E	R	A	L	D	E	62 A	R	R	I	63 N	64 G	65 S
66 E	R	R		67 L	E	I		68 C	E	O		69 O	U	R
70 E	T	A		71 I	C	E		72 T	E	N		73 G	T	O

🌴 Belle's Gift To Rosco 🌴

1:I	2:Q	3:S	█	4:A	5:F	6:T	█	7:I	8:R	9:T	█	10:S	11:M	12:L
13:N	U	T	█	14:R	O	D	█	15:R	E	O	█	16:T	O	E
17:D	E	A	18:R	R	O	S	19:C	O	M	Y	20:L	O	V	E
21:R	E	T	O	O	L	█	22:U	N	O	█	23:E	R	I	K
24:I	G	O	T	W	H	25:A	T	I	T	26:T	A	K	E	S
█	█	█	27:S	E	C	█	28:C	E	E	█	█	█	█	█
29:I	30:T	31:S	32:A	█	33:A	34:D	D	█	35:S	36:A	37:L	38:A	39:D	S
40:F	A	T	H	41:E	R	C	H	42:R	I	S	T	M	A	S
43:S	T	U	A	R	T	█	44:L	A	G	█	45:D	O	N	T
█	█	█	46:G	Y	47:P	█	48:C	N	49:N	█	█	█	█	█
50:O	51:N	52:E	53:L	O	V	E	54:L	Y	P	A	55:I	56:R	57:O	58:F
59:P	A	I	R	█	60:I	C	E	█	61:O	P	T	I	M	A
62:I	C	E	H	63:O	C	K	E	Y	64:S	K	A	T	E	S
65:U	R	I	█	66:W	E	E	█	67:O	T	I	█	68:A	N	T
69:M	E	O	█	70:L	S	D	█	71:U	S	N	█	72:S	S	S